MW01243053

Devon's Deal

STEPHANIE RENEE

Copyright © by Stephanie Renee

All rights reserved.

No portion of this book may be reproduced in any form without written permission from the publisher or author, except as permitted by U.S. copyright law.

This book has a very large, very anxiety-ridden Doberman within its pages. Bones is based off of Knuckles, our sweet Dobie that we lost unexpectedly earlier this year. He was the sweetest boy, and I knew he had to be immortalized in one of my books.
Never forget to hug your fur babies.

Chapter One

DEVON

"What the hell do you mean I can't bring a date?" I ask, not trying to hide my annoyance. "It's a wedding, Becky."

"Exactly, Devon," she defends with a heavy dose of sass. "Which means we need to know the definite number of people who are going to be there."

I turn to Dan, the lucky groom in this situation and my best friend since I was five. "Come on, man."

"Sorry, Dev. The wedding is all Becky's thing. She's the one you need to convince."

"Dan, isn't it supposed to be bros before—"

Becky cuts me off. "Don't you dare finish that sentence."

Holding up my hands, I say, "Okay, sorry."

She sets her hands on the table in front of her, interlocking her fingers. "Look, Devon, here's the deal. You and Kyra were supposed to come

1

together, but you broke up. It happens. I know how you two are—on again, off again—so I waited as long as I could to see if you'd get back together. But we're getting down to the wire, and I need to give the venue exact numbers. The wedding itself wouldn't be a big deal, but the entire wedding party has the venue booked for almost a week beforehand. They need a definitive count."

Just the mention of Kyra's name makes my jaw clench. After me kissing her ass, trying to make our relationship work for three years, we finally decided to call it quits.

She decided to call it quits.

Our plan was to go to this wedding together as a romantic getaway. Now, apparently, I have to go alone.

That's just not going to work for me.

Not sure I want to know the answer, I still ask, "Is Kyra bringing a date?"

They exchange a sympathetic glance between the two of them, letting me know all I need to.

"I guess that's a yes," I mumble. "If she can bring a date, why can't I?"

"Well," Dan begins, but Becky doesn't let him get any further.

"Because it's not just a date she's bringing. It's her boyfriend. You don't have a girlfriend...or anything remotely close. All you've had is a string of women that you've had meaningless sex with. I don't see you bringing any of them on a week-long trip."

"You don't think I could find someone to bring?" I ask.

"Do I think you could pay a woman to come with you? Sure. Heck, you could probably even sweet talk one of your floozies into coming, but I don't want some easy bimbo at my wedding in all the photos."

But it's fine for Kyra's boyfriend to be in your precious pictures?

"Becky, has it ever occurred to you that I don't have a girlfriend because I don't *want* one, not because I can't get one?"

That gets a loud scoff out of her. "I don't think those two things are mutually exclusive."

"Your wedding is still six months away! I'm sure I can find a girlfriend by then."

Dan finally pipes up. "Honey, six months *is* a long time. It may be better to give him a plus one now than for him not to have one later. His future girlfriend may be offended that she wasn't invited."

She purses her lips together. "His *imaginary* girlfriend?"

Realizing he's fighting a losing battle, Dan decides to shut his mouth.

Becky turns her attention back to me. "Look, I'm not trying to be a Bridezilla here."

Could have fooled me.

She continues, "My parents are footing the bill for this wedding, and I don't want them paying unnecessary expenses."

"I'm the best man! Me having a date is unnecessary? I'm going to look really pathetic if I'm there alone."

Dan says, "You could always hook up with a bridesmaid." He starts laughing but immediately stops when he sees Becky's face.

"No, he can't, Daniel. All of them already have dates...or husbands."

Realizing I'm not getting anywhere, I decide to try some good old-fashioned begging. "Come on, Beck. Tell me what it'll take. I'll do anything."

Most times, I would enjoy being a single guy at a wedding. As Dan pointed out, it's not a bad place to meet women. But I refuse to go on this week-long affair alone. Maybe it's sheer pettiness, but I don't want to be the sad bachelor while Kyra has a date.

I watch Becky as she thinks in absolute silence. She'll probably tell me to fuck off. When Kyra and I were together, the four of us hung out all the time. Becky tolerated me better back then. Now, I'm just her fiancé's annoying single friend.

"I'll make you a deal," she finally says.

"Alright, hit me with it."

"If you can find a girlfriend—not just a date—by the wedding, you can bring her. And you can't just pretend to have someone be your girlfriend. I want to see you having a real-genuine connection with someone. The sparks better be flying."

"Easy," I say, my confidence overflowing.

She points her finger at me. "BUT if you can't find a girlfriend, you will fork over the money that was paid for the extra guest."

"Okay, how much is that?" I ask.

"Two thousand dollars."

My mouth drops. I knew Becky's family was well-off, but I had no idea they were two-grand-a-person rich.

When she sees the look on my face, she says, "Now, you know why I need a definitive count for the guest list."

I should probably back out of this whole thing. I don't exactly have two grand lying around. But I've come this far and already dug my heels in. I'm nothing if not stubborn.

I sit quietly for a moment while my pride and my logic play a mental tug-of-war inside my brain.

Becky finally asks, "So, do we have a deal?"

I know there's only one choice.

"Absolutely."

After all, the wedding is six months away.

How hard can it be to find a girlfriend by then?

Chapter Two

DEVON

Six months later.

"So, let me get this straight," my younger brother, Tanner, begins. "You guaranteed your friends that you would have a girlfriend to take to the wedding, or you would pay them two grand?"

"That about sums it up," I say before sipping my beer.

Our older brother, Duke, chimes in. "And you haven't managed to find a girlfriend in six months?"

"I'm totally fucked," I mutter.

I called both of my brothers to come out with me to my favorite bar, The Crazy Horse, to try to help me figure this whole thing out.

They both start laughing, and Duke asks, "Why can't you find a girl? You're dating all the time."

Tanner mumbles, "You use the word *dating* very loosely."

I should probably be offended, but he's not wrong. Since Kyra and I broke up, I've been doing the exact opposite of settling down.

"Look, I've been a little distracted," I defend.

Tanner says, "Yeah, by every cute piece of tail within a five-town radius."

"What can I say? I like to have fun."

Duke leans back in his chair. "Okay, this may seem obvious, but word around town is that you're a decent lay. Why not just ask one of the girls you've slept with to be your date?"

Confusion clouds my face. "Decent? Who said I'm only decent?"

All of us start laughing. I finally say, "Most of them were just a one-night thing. I made it pretty clear that was as much as I was willing to give. I'd feel like a complete hypocrite if I called them asking to pretend to be my girlfriend."

"You could either be a hypocrite or be broke," Tanner says. "Either way, you're fucked."

I roll my eyes. "Thank you, Captain Obvious. You two have it easy. You're both married. Hey, can I borrow one of your wives?"

They both give a stern, "No."

Duke met his wife a couple years ago while he did work on a house she inherited. And Tanner met his at a bar when she was singing karaoke. They're both so happy it's cute...and slightly nauseating.

Lucky bastards.

I never thought I'd be jealous of their domestic lives, but here we are.

Tanner says, "Okay, let's think. The three of us can come up with something."

I chug the rest of the beer in my bottle. "Give it up, man. I think I'm a hopeless cause."

He looks at me. "Do you have two thousand dollars?"

"You're right. I think we can put our heads together and think of something."

Duke asks, "So, are there any women in town that you haven't slept with?"

Tanner says, "If they've got any sense, there are."

"Shut up," I tell him. "I haven't slept with every girl in town."

Just a lot of them.

Duke looks back and forth between the two of us. "I think we are going to need more beer. I'll get the next round."

He stands up and heads to the bar. Tanner turns to me. "Dude, why is this so important to you?"

"What do you mean?"

"I mean, under normal circumstances, you would love going to a wedding alone. You'd get more tail than you'd know what to do with."

"Why do you keep referring to it as *tail?* When did that start?"

"Come on, Dev. What's going on?"

I pick at the label on my beer bottle. "Kyra's going to be there."

"So?"

"So, it's my first time seeing her since the break-up."

His eyes go wide. "No shit?"

"I've made every attempt to avoid her, but that won't be possible at this wedding. It's either I go by myself and watch Kyra and her new boyfriend for a whole week, or I find myself a date."

He nods. "Got it."

Duke appears back at the table with three beers in hand. "Hey, what about the bartender?"

I look to see who's working tonight. "Shay? What about her?"

He looks at me like I'm an idiot. "Why don't you ask her to be your date for the wedding?"

Tanner's eyebrows raise. "That would be an interesting match. The golden retriever who tries to hump everything meets the black cat who hates everyone."

"She doesn't hate everyone," I say.

But I guess I get why he would think that. Shay Baxter has the type of aura that warns people to stay the fuck away. And her dark sense of humor and biting wit aren't for everyone.

Tanner gives a small smile. "So, you two talk?"

"Yeah. In case you haven't noticed, I come in here quite a bit."

Duke jumps in. "You haven't slept with her, have you?"

Tanner laughs. "No, I don't think Shay is his type."

"Why not?" Duke asks.

"Yeah, why not?" I echo.

He points to the bar. "That woman is literally the exact opposite of Kyra."

He's not wrong. Kyra is tall and thin where Shay is shorter and has curves. Kyra is obsessed with clothes and liked showing as much skin as possible. Shay typically wears jeans and black t-shirts with rock bands on them. Kyra is the definition of the word *preppy*...while Shay is...goth? Alternative? Punk? I don't know, but it's the opposite of preppy.

Although different, I don't think either type is better than the other. Each is attractive in her own right.

"I don't have a type," I say. "I date all kinds of women."

Tanner says, "Dude, she'd eat you alive in the bedroom."

"Oh, I doubt that."

I'd be the one doing the eating.

Duke asks, "Why not ask her? You already seem to have some type of relationship with her."

It's not a horrible idea, but there's just one problem.

I take another sip of beer. "I can't."

"Why not?" Duke presses.

"Because she asked me to come help her put in new counters and cabinets in her kitchen. I told her I would, but I keep putting it off."

"Oh, dude," Tanner says. "Why haven't you done it?"

"I do carpentry all day long. When I get off, I like doing other things."

"Or other women." Tanner rolls his eyes.

Duke says, "Sounds like you've got some leverage."

"What do you mean?" I ask.

"I'd say it's a *great* time to do Shay's kitchen, and I think you're going to do it for *free*."

"Free?" I question. "Why? She was going to pay me."

Tanner asks, "Was it more than two grand?"

Duke continues, "If you do this, it gives her some incentive to help you out."

Looking at him, I can't believe he's so invested in this. Five years ago, you couldn't pay my big brother to get involved in anyone else's business.

I say, "I'm not sure if Avery's been a good influence on you or a bad one."

He swigs his beer. "Oh, I think we both know the answer to that."

Tanner says, "Duke has a point. Maybe Shay isn't a bad idea. I guess she isn't the *best* either, but you're out of options unless you want to travel to Arizona."

"Texas is a big place," I argue.

"Not big enough. Now, go talk to her."

"Can I finish my beer first?"

Tanner takes the bottle out of my hand and chugs down what's left. "There. All gone. Looks like you need another."

Both of them stare at me intently until I finally get up from the table. As I walk to the bar, I hope Shay is busy with customers so that I have a reason to delay embarrassing myself.

But no such luck.

She's wiping down the bar top.

"Hey, Sunshine," I greet, taking a seat on one of the stools.

"Well, if it isn't the middle Samson brother. How's it going, Cassanova?" Her nickname for me has always made me chuckle. "Another beer?"

"Yeah, please."

As she walks to the cooler, I take the time to really look at her. She wears her typical ripped skinny jeans, baggy black t-shirt, and old Chuck Taylors. Her hair is platinum blonde, almost a white shade. It's parted off to one side and hangs just below her chin. Her hazel eyes are accentuated by dark eyeshadow and black eyeliner. And she has two small piercings—one in her nose and one in the side of her bottom lip. I think she has her tongue pierced too.

Setting the beer on the counter, she asks, "Do you want me to put it on Duke's tab?"

I smile. "Absolutely."

When I don't immediately get up and walk away, she asks, "Aren't you going back to your brothers?"

We both turn to look at Tanner and Duke who are staring directly back at us.

Shay asks, "Why are they being so weird?"

"Oh, they're just bored," I mutter. "But I actually wanted to talk to you about something."

"Okay?" She leans her elbows on the bar. "About what?"

"I was thinking maybe this weekend, I could come over and start on your kitchen."

"Oh, that would be great. Did you figure out how much you think it'll cost?"

I nervously tap my fingers on the lacquered wood of the bar. "Well, maybe I could do it for free."

"Free? What's your game, Samson?"

"What do you mean?"

"I mean, you've been putting me off for weeks now. All of a sudden, you're eager to do it for no pay? Bullshit. What do you want?"

I should've known Shay would see right through me. She's the most no-nonsense woman I've ever met. "Alright, alright." Taking a deep breath, I continue, "I have a proposition for you."

Chapter Three

SHAY

"Okay, just so I understand this—you want me to come on a week-long wedding with you and pretend to be your girlfriend?" I ask in sheer disbelief.

"Yeah, that pretty much sums it up."

"And in return, you're going to help me remodel my kitchen for free?"

"Yep. I'll even foot the bill for any of the materials you don't already have."

Damn. Now, I wish I wouldn't have already bought almost everything.

I look him up and down. His light blue eyes look at me from under the brim of one of the baseball caps he's always wearing. A few strands of his chestnut brown hair that's a little longer on top hang out from underneath. He's got cute little dimples, but they aren't always visible with his constant stubble. And the way he smiles makes me fully aware of why so many girls go home with him.

Which brings me to my next question: why is he asking me to do this? Devon Samson has absolutely no trouble finding women to spend time with him. I've seen him pick up enough of them in this very bar. He's good-looking, confident, and a real charmer. So, why strike a deal with me?

Someone walks to the bar, so I point to him and say, "Hold that thought."

I make three different frozen drinks for the woman and get back to Devon as quickly as I can. Not wanting to get distracted again, I tell the other bartender, Suzie, I'm going to take my break.

"Devon, let's go talk outside," I say.

Once we are out in the Texas heat, I walk over and take a seat at one of the outdoor tables.

"Geez," Devon says. "It's October. You'd think it would start to cool down a little."

I give a tiny laugh, but I'd like to stop the small talk.

"Devon, why are you asking me to do this?"

"Would you believe me if I said it was your sparkling wit and bubbly personality?"

"Absolutely fucking not."

He adjusts the baseball cap on his head. "Yeah, I didn't think so."

"Devon, my break is only fifteen minutes long. Let's cut the bullshit."

He looks at me. "I need you not to take offense to this, but you're sort of...my last option."

"Man, you know how to make a girl feel special," I joke.

"I'm sorry. That sounds really bad. I'm just between a rock and a hard place here."

He looks at me with those gorgeous blue eyes that all the Samson boys share.

Exhaling a heavy sigh, I ask, "What would I have to do?"

A glimpse of hope crosses his face. "You'd spend the week pretending to be my girlfriend."

"Would I have to sleep with you?" It sounds like a ridiculous question, but as a bartender, I've learned that you have to make the lines perfectly clear when it comes to men.

He chuckles. "I mean, I wouldn't say no to that, but no, it's not a requirement. I won't pressure you into anything."

"But we will have to act like a couple? Probably means kissing and holding hands, right?"

His lips pull into a crooked smile. "Well, we have to make it look believable."

If I'm being honest, doing any of those things with Devon doesn't completely repulse me. Although not my normal type, the middle Samson brother is *really* fun to look at.

"And if I do this, you're going to finally help me redo my kitchen?"

He nods. "Absolutely."

I think for a moment, not believing I'm actually considering this. This is my life, not the plot of a rom-com. But it's not like I have a lot of other things going on. I consider myself a bit of an adrenaline junkie, and I could use some excitement. Everything has been a bit stale lately.

I ask, "How do I know you won't just ghost me after this whole thing is over?"

"Well, Shay, we live in a pretty small town. You *do* know where I live. But if it'll make you feel better, I'll get started on it before we leave. I'll even leave my tools at your house. You can hold them hostage until the job's finished."

"I do like the sound of that," I giggle. "But I'll have to take a whole week off work."

I leave out the part about having a shit ton of vacation time to burn. I want to see how much he's willing to sweeten the deal.

"Come on, you could use some time off. You're here all the time. Everything will be covered all week long. Food. Drinks. Your room. All taken care of. And of course, if anything else should come up, I'll handle it."

"It kind of makes me feel like a call girl or something." I chew on my bottom lip. "That should probably bother me more than it does."

"If it's too much to ask, I understand."

I take another minute to think and consider my options. Most would think it's crazy to do something like this, but I don't tend to follow most social norms. I don't know why this should be any different.

Plus, getting my kitchen done for free is a definite perk since I'm trying to save money.

"Okay, Devon. I'll do this on one condition."

"Hit me with it."

"Tell me why. And don't give me some bullshit cutesy answer, and don't be all cryptic. Tell me the truth."

"You sure you want to know? It doesn't make me look great."

I shrug my shoulders. "Tell me anyway."

He looks at his hands, rubbing them together while he starts to speak. "I sort of made a bet with the bride that I would be able to find a girlfriend for this thing. I've done a shit job at it, so I either find a fake date, or I have to pay the cost of my extra guest—which is two thousand dollars."

Holy hell. Who pays two grand a person at a wedding?

A bet may sound like a stupid reason to most, but I can get on board with that way quicker than some other reasons.

"So, this whole thing is a bet?" I ask.

His embarrassment is clear. "Yeah."

I smile. "Why didn't you just say that?"

Chapter Four

SHAY

"I'm sorry, but this whole thing just seems crazy to me," Suzie begins. "Devon Samson wants you to be his date for a wedding for an entire week?"

"Yep," I reply, folding a t-shirt and adding to the stack I've already done.

Suzie and I both managed to get the same day off, and how are we spending it? She's hanging out here while I catch up on laundry.

My giant Doberman, Bones, sits down next to Suzie, leaning his big black and tan body into hers. He holds up one paw and just stares at her.

"What's wrong with this dog?" Suzie asks, pointing to him.

"He wants you to hold his paw."

"Why?"

"Because he's co-dependent and anxiety ridden. Just hold his paw and deal with it."

She takes his large paw in her hand as they just sit and stare at each other for a moment. Without warning, the dog flops down, laying in a heap in Suzie's lap.

She laughs. "A big scary guard dog who is secretly a giant softy."

"Get used to it. He'll be your best friend the week I'm gone."

"And we have to stay here? Why can't he come stay at my place?"

I look at her. "Did you not hear the part about him having anxiety?"

Her eyes roll while she scratches Bones on the top of his head. "Oh, right."

I smile. "But he'll keep you safe here."

"Alright, alright," she concedes as the dog nuzzles against her. As she looks around at all the folded clothes, she asks, "When was the last time you did laundry?"

"Let's just say I ran out of clean underwear over a week ago, and I've been going commando since."

"You know if you did a load every couple days, maybe that wouldn't happen."

"Hey, maybe I like going commando. The girl needs to breathe every now and then."

She laughs. "Now, let's get back to your little arrangement with Devon Samson."

"I know it sounds crazy, but he's going to redo my kitchen for free. That seems like a pretty decent reason."

She purses her lips together. "Oh, I can think of another reason."

"What are you talking about?"

"Oh, don't pretend like you don't know what his nickname around town is."

"Nickname?"

She leans forward and covers the dog's ears. Popping her gum, she says, "Devon Samson is known by the fairer sex as Mr. Pussy."

"Mr.—"

"Pussy. Every girl around town he's been with says he loves *giving* more than *receiving*. He loves eating pussy. And every one of those girls says he's amazing at it."

Truth be told, I have heard the rumors. I'm a bartender. I hear *all* the rumors, but I try to regard them as just that—rumors.

"You actually put stock into that?" I ask.

"You know those baseball caps he's always wearing?"

I nod.

"You know he means business when he flips it backwards. Makes it easier for him to really get in there and do the job right, if you know what I mean."

"Yeah, I get what you mean, but it doesn't mean it's true. Lots of men think they're good at it, but really, they suck."

Suzie blows a bubble with her gum. "It's not like he's going around saying it. It's the women he's been with."

"The many, *many* women," I say with a heavy dose of sarcasm.

She points her finger at me. "Let's not pretend you haven't let your fair share of questionable cocks into your hen house."

"Hey," I quip. "Not in front of the dog. Besides, we aren't talking about me. People aren't coming into the bar, gossiping about my sex life."

"Really, Miss Pierced Nipples?"

My mouth drops open. "Okay, maybe they have." *At least they left my clit piercing out of it.*

"Look, Shay, all I'm saying is maybe you could see if the rumors are true. You guys will be staying in the same room for a whole week. Let me live vicariously through you."

Honestly, the thought has crossed my mind. Do I *plan* on sleeping with Devon? No. But I wouldn't be complaining if it happened. I'm always up for a good roll in the sheets.

Does that make me sound bad?

Eh, it is what it is.

Suzie gets my attention again. "How does Travis feel about you going away with another man for a week?"

"We ended things a few weeks ago."

"What? Why?"

I play with my lip ring. "Because we ran out of things to talk about when we had our clothes on. We just didn't have a lot in common."

In other words, it was boring. There was no connection.

"I'm sorry, Shay. Why didn't you tell me?"

"Because it wasn't a big deal. Nothing about our relationship was a big deal."

She rolls her eyes, so I ask, "What was that for?"

"You could be in a perfect relationship with the perfect guy, and you'd still say it was no big deal. You never get invested in anything, and you haven't since—"

I cut her off because I don't even want to hear that name.

"Exactly. If you don't care, you don't get hurt."

"Have you ever considered a career making those motivational posters?" She jokes.

"Oh, yes. Right after I become a debutante."

She smiles. "I can't wait to see you in one of those puffy dresses. Speaking of which, what are you supposed to wear to this thing?"

I gesture to all the clean laundry. "I'll pick out seven pairs of jeans and seven t-shirts."

"Shay, this is a *wedding*."

"So? I'll pick out the nicer stuff."

"Uh, no. You can't wear any of this. You need to look halfway decent. Plus, you're supposed to pose as Devon's girlfriend, right?"

I nod.

"Have you seen the type of girl Devon goes out with?"

"Yeah, and his tastes really run the gambit," I retort.

"But none of them have been all *princess of darkness* like you."

"Hey, I don't wear black lipstick anymore," I defend.

"Still, you know what I mean."

"Suzie, it's not like I have a lot of dress clothes. I never need them. I'm working all the fucking time."

"You used to go to the club a lot."

I laugh. "If you think my normal clothes are inappropriate for a wedding, wait until you see my club clothes."

Careful not to disturb Bones, who has now started to fall asleep, Suzie reaches over to grab a pair of my underwear. "Do you really intend on wearing these?" she asks in disbelief.

"What on God's green Earth is wrong with my underwear?"

"What if Mr. Pussy decides he wants to take a trip *downtown?* Do you really want to be caught in these?"

"They've never been an issue before. I find most men don't care as much about the panties as what's underneath."

She sets the pair back down. "Whatever you say."

She pauses a moment before asking, "So, what all will you be doing on this trip? A week seems like a hell of a long time for a wedding."

"I have no idea. Devon's supposed to come start on the kitchen later tonight, and I'll pick his brain some more."

"Mm-hmm," she mumbles. "You better ask if there's a dress code."

I start to wonder if this whole thing is a terrible idea.

Oh well. That's never stopped me before.

Chapter Five

DEVON

"Come on in," Shay calls from the other side of her screen door.

I walk through with my bag of tools in hand into her living room. I expect to see Shay standing there, but instead, I find a hundred-pound Doberman silently staring at me.

He doesn't growl.

He doesn't bark.

I think this is worse.

I can't tell what he's thinking.

"Uhhhh...Shay," I call. "There's some sort of Hellhound in your living room."

She walks in from the hallway and sees her dog. "Oh, sorry. I thought he was still eating." When she stands next to him, she gently lays his hand on his head and says, "Stand down, Bones. Devon's cool."

Instantly, his entire demeanor changes. He goes from completely immobile and scary to wagging his nubby little tail.

I take a deep breath, trying to get my heart to settle down. "Shay, why am I not surprised you have a Doberman as your dog?"

She smiles. "You know I have absolutely nothing to worry about at night."

Honestly, I doubt Shay has much to worry about with or without the dog. She may be short in stature, but I have a feeling she could defend herself.

"Come on," she says. "Let's go to the kitchen."

I follow her and the dog trailing at her side. After passing through the doorway, I halt at the sight before me. Shay's cabinets are all mangled. Most of the doors have been ripped off. One side hangs on by nothing more than a few splinters, and there are giant holes in the wood.

"Shay, did you try to take these down by yourself?"

She crosses her arms over her chest and looks over her handywork. "Yeah. Turns out you need more than just a sledgehammer. Now, I just take a few swings when I've had a bad day."

"Remind me not to piss you off," I mumble.

I get to work, starting to take down what's left of the cabinets.

"Do you want some coffee?" Shay asks. "I just made a fresh pot."

I glance at the clock on the wall. "It's almost eight at night."

"So?"

"So, don't you think it's a bit late?"

"I'm a bartender. Being a night owl is kind of a requirement."

I nod. "Right. Sure, a cup of coffee sounds great."

I'd normally say no since I have to get up for work at the ass crack of dawn, but I may as well since I'm going to be here working for a little while.

She pours me a mug and sets it on the small kitchen table before grabbing cream and sugar and setting them down as well. I watch her take a sip from her own cup without adding anything to it.

"You drink it black?" I ask, pouring cream into mine.

Without looking at me, she replies, "Just like my soul."

I walk around the kitchen before peeking back in to see the living room. Looking at Shay's house, I see it's much more warm and inviting than I would have imagined. She'd shown me photos of the kitchen when she originally asked for my help, but they didn't really give the full picture.

"Your house isn't quite what I was expecting," I tell her.

That gets her to look at me. "What were you expecting? Black walls? Chains and whips? Leather?"

I laugh. "Something like that."

The corner of her mouth pulls into a smirk. "Well, you haven't seen my bedroom."

I just sip my coffee because I have no idea if she's kidding or not. Is it hotter if she is or isn't?

27

As if she sees my wheels turning, she says, "Just a joke, Devon. I like my house to have a homey feel to it. If I want whips and chains, they make clubs for that."

Once again, no idea if she's serious.

Thankfully, she changes the subject. "What all are we doing this next week? It seems like an awfully long time for wedding festivities."

I pull out my phone to look at the email Becky sent me a couple of days ago. When I confidently told her I was bringing my *girlfriend,* Shay, she scoffed and gave a cocky, "We'll see."

Reading over the list, I say, "The first night, we can't check in until after four, but then, they're having a little welcome dinner for everyone." Skimming further, I continue. "We've got a pool day, some spa time, bachelor and bachelorette parties, the rehearsal dinner, and the wedding itself."

"Geez." She sighs. "That's a lot."

"Yeah, the majority of the wedding party lives out of town, so I think they're trying to fit it all in while everyone's in the same place. But rest assured, I know Becky, and she'll make sure everything is the best of the best. And there will be an open bar all week."

She grins. "You should've led with that."

I get back to work on the cabinets while Shay busies herself straightening up. I catch glimpses of her chewing on her bottom lip as she walks by. I wonder what it would be like to kiss that lip of hers—to pull it between my own and nibble on it. I don't know why because I've never thought of Shay like that before.

Okay, that's a lie. I'm a guy. I feel like we are hardwired to have the occasional dirty thought about the women we interact with. But I've never made a habit out of it with Shay. In fact, normally when I'm around her, I'm on a date with another girl...or I'm trying to find one to go home with.

Shay has always been the hot, badass bartender that has been someone I deemed off-limits—mainly because I haven't wanted things to get weird with the person who serves me drinks at my favorite watering hole.

I'm pretty sure that after our upcoming trip, though, a line will be crossed—especially if I can't stop doing things like picturing biting her lip.

I meant when I said I wouldn't push her into anything, though.

She will call all the shots this week—even if I'm out two grand. I'll never be the man who forces a woman to do something she's not completely comfortable with.

But fuck, my cock hopes that she wants more. I don't know if it's pure curiosity, the fact that she's hot as sin, or that I know I won't be getting any for a week. Maybe a combination of all three.

Something about Shay intrigues me. Nobody around town seems to know much about her—at least not that I've heard. Then again, I haven't really asked either. She and I have always had some laughs and decent banter, but besides that, she's been a mystery. I'd like to get to know her better during this trip. Lord knows, we will have enough time to do that.

"Can I ask you something, Shay?"

"I can't guarantee I'll answer but go for it."

I walk over to take another drink of coffee. "Why did you agree to this? I mean, I'm sure you have better things to do than a favor for me."

"Is it considered a favor when you're doing my kitchen?" She asks.

"Come on, Shay," I say. "That can't be the only reason."

Her shoulders give a heavy shrug. "A little trip away doesn't sound half bad. Plus, I wouldn't want you to lose two grand. How will you tip me when I serve you drinks if you're in the poor house?"

I chuckle. "I appreciate that." I pause for a moment, knowing I need to come clean about something. "There's one more thing about this week that I need you to know."

"Alright?"

"My ex is going to be at this thing. Kyra. We were together a few years and were pretty serious before having a messy breakup. I just didn't want you to be blindsided when we get there."

She thinks for a moment, shaking her hair out of her face. "Why'd you break up?"

"She broke up with me. We were on again, off again for a while. I kept trying to make it work, but she left and made it very clear she wasn't coming back."

Saying it out loud makes me sound kind of pathetic.

Shay's blue eyes look up to stare right through me. "Are you still in love with her? Do you want her back?"

"No," I answer matter-of-factly. "She took our dog."

"Huh?"

"We adopted a dog together. Bruno. She took him when she left, and I haven't seen him since."

Shay's forehead scrunches up. "What a bitch."

"Fair warning, she's probably going to be an even bigger bitch to you this week. Kyra isn't known for playing well with others."

"I can handle myself," Shay defends.

"Oh, I don't doubt that. I just don't want you to be caught off guard."

"I'll be alright. I always am."

"Full disclosure, Shay, part of the reason I didn't want to go alone is that I didn't want to be the sad single guy while she was there with her boyfriend." I don't know why I'm telling her this, but here we are.

I add, "Man, I'm not coming off great here, am I?"

"Devon, I'm no saint. You won't get any judgement from me. I understand the feeling of wanting to stick it to your ex."

"Well, thanks," I say, standing up to get back to work.

"Hey, Dev, what's the dress code for this thing?"

"Let's just say I've been told that my baseball cap won't be acceptable at a good amount of the functions."

She lets out a long groan. "That's what I was afraid of."

She pulls out her phone, and I ask what she's doing.

"Calling in reinforcements."

Chapter Six

SHAY

"Will you get out here?" One of my dads calls from outside the dressing room.

"No," I answer defiantly. "This dress has flowers on it."

"So?"

"And it's yellow."

"Shay Alexandra, get out here."

I roll my eyes so hard that I'm surprised I can't see my brain, but I still open the door and walk out.

My two dads stand there, looking me up and down. Pops has a blank look on his face, not giving me any hint of what he's thinking. Dad, on the other hand, looks so giddy he may burst.

He squeals, "Look at you! I haven't seen you in a cute yellow dress since you were old enough to say the word *no.*"

"Don't get used to it," I tell him. "I'm not getting it."

"Oh, I know." He lifts his phone to snap a quick photo. "Just wanted to get some blackmail."

"Of course," I mutter before walking back into the dressing room. "Look, I get that I have to dress up for this thing, but don't they have anything that's a little more my style?"

Seconds later, a new stack of dresses is slung over the dressing room door. "I thought you might ask that."

These all seem to be much more aligned with my tastes.

Dark colors? Check.

No flowers? Check.

I slide the first one on. Even though it's black, I'm still a bit out of my comfort zone. I don't mind my body or my curves. I've always embraced them. But I don't typically show them off.

I've been a bartender for the better part of ten years. As much as showing some skin helps my tips, it also garners a lot of unwanted and unwelcome attention. Sometimes, it's better to just cover up.

Plus, jeans and t-shirts are way more comfortable.

Unfortunately, I don't think those are going to be an option for the next week.

I look myself up and down once again. I may feel a little silly, but I look pretty good.

"Well?" Dad asks.

Pops shooshes him. "Give her a minute."

"Well, she's taking forever."

Pops laughs. "You're really enjoying this, aren't you?"

"Are you kidding? Our daughter hasn't let us take her shopping in years, and every time before that, it was under extreme protest. I'm *living* for this moment right now."

I speak up. "You know I can hear you two, right?"

Dad replies, "Yeah, yeah. Hurry up."

The next two hours are spent with me parading in and out of the dressing room, trying on what I'm convinced is every single dress in the store. If it was a movie, this is where a montage to a Madonna song would happen.

Wanting this whole thing to be over, I settle on some dresses, some leggings, a couple of nice shirts, and a skirt.

Good lord, what have I become?

I'm grateful at the end of this journey because shopping happens to be one of my least favorite activities—unless I'm on my computer in the comfort of my living room.

When I'm back in my own clothing, I'm ready to move on to more fun things. But Dad has other plans.

"Okay, now, let's go look at shoes."

The hits just keep on coming.

"You know that's your third margarita," Pops says to Dad. "We haven't even gotten our food yet."

Dad shrugs his shoulders. "Shopping makes me thirsty."

Pops laughs. "Shay, you and I are going to have to cart him out of here in a wheelbarrow."

I scoop salsa from the bowl in the middle of the table onto a tortilla chip. "If I keep eating these, I might need a wheelbarrow too."

People have always asked if it was weird growing up with two dads and no mom. Sure, being from a small town got us a fair amount of dirty looks and harsh whispers, but I never felt like I was missing out on anything. I have two awesome men in my corner who love me more than anything. They taught me how to ride a bike and how to stand up for myself. They bought me my first training bra and tampons when I needed them. I could always talk to them about anything.

Still can.

Dad asks, "So, do you think you have everything you need for the wedding?"

"I think so." I leave out the part of how I may take Suzie's advice and buy some new underwear.

I love my dads, but now that I'm thirty, I don't really want to shop for *those* with them.

Going on, I say, "Thank you two for coming with me. I don't think I would have been very good at picking out clothes outside my comfort zone. Girly isn't really my thing."

Dad rolls his eyes. "Oh, hold on. Let me put on my shocked face."

Pops joins in. "Remember when she was little, and we thought she was outside picking flowers, and she ended up bringing a snake inside the house instead?"

I practically bark, "You guys didn't even give him a chance!"

Dad cries, "Shay, he bit my toe! I still have the scar! You didn't even tell us you were bringing him inside!"

"I had a shoebox for him."

"Shay, the thing was three feet long."

I wave my hand. "Eh, semantics."

We all start laughing and are only interrupted when our food arrives.

Pops scoops sour cream onto his tacos as he asks, "So, tell us more about this guy that you're going to this wedding with. Are you sure he's not your boyfriend?"

"Nope. Not my boyfriend," I reply.

Confused, Dad asks, "Is he just some stranger?"

"No, he comes to the bar a lot. I guess you call us friends—just not close ones."

Pops questions, "So, you're just going to go to a wedding with this guy for a whole week?"

"Yeah. Why not? Gives me a reason to take off work and gets my kitchen done for free."

Dad smiles. "I love how you just fly through life by the seat of your pants. I could never be so impulsive."

Pops lets out a heavy scoff. "Tell that to our credit card."

Dad looks at him with wide eyes. "Next, I'll buy you a lovely doghouse you can sleep in." Turning his attention back to me, he asks, "Is this guy cute?"

"Devon? Yeah, he's not bad to look at."

Dad leans close to Pops and whispers, "That means she thinks he's *really* cute."

"Oh, hush," I tell him.

Does Devon have gorgeous blue eyes and brown hair that's just the perfect amount of messy? Yes. But I'm not about to tell them that.

"How's everything else been going?" Pops asks. "I feel like I haven't seen much of you lately."

"I'm sorry. I've been working a lot—trying to save up for a bigger stake in the bar."

Right now, I own fifteen percent of the bar I work at. Gill, the owner, is wanting to retire in the next few years. I begged him to let me buy it, but since I was a broke bitch, we worked out a plan to let me purchase small amounts of equity at a time.

Dad says, "I wish you'd let us help. We could lend you the money, so you wouldn't have to work yourself to death."

Pops speaks before I can. "Oh, leave her alone, Rich. It's good that our daughter has such a strong work ethic."

"I like working," I defend. "I like keeping busy, and I'm sure it'll mean more to me if I earn it all myself."

Pops smiles. "And we are *very* proud of you."

Dad agrees. "Of course, we are! You know I'll just always worry about you, no matter how old you are. I wish you would have at least let us pay for your clothes, though."

"Dad, I'm old enough to buy my own clothes."

"Fine." He purses his lips together. "But *we* are paying for dinner. Now, when do you leave for this trip?"

"Tomorrow."

"Why am I not surprised you're waiting until the last possible second to do your shopping?" He sighs.

"Would you expect anything else from me?" I grin.

Dad says, "Not at all. And I hope you have fun next week. Just please be careful. It's easy to get caught up in your feelings even in a *fake* relationship. I don't want you to get hurt."

I know he's just looking out for me. They both are. But they really don't need to worry. It takes a whole hell of a lot for me to catch feelings for someone. I doubt that a single week away is going to change that.

"I'll be careful," I assure him. "You know me."

His eyes flick up from his plate to look at me. "I do. That's why I'm saying it."

"I'll be fine. We're just going to have some fun and let off some steam. No harm, no foul."

And I mean it. I know who I am, and I know the giant walls I've put up around myself. I'm not coming out of this week with anything more than a new kitchen.

There's no way I'm going to do something stupid like fall in love.

No way in hell.

Chapter Seven

DEVON

"Hey, you ready to go?" I ask Shay as she holds open her screen door for me.

"I think so. Just give me a minute."

Bones walks over to me and sniffs my hand before letting me pet the top of his head. He's not so scary when he's being nice.

Shay walks around frantically, trying to make sure she hasn't forgotten anything.

A woman emerges from the kitchen, and I recognize her as Suzie, one of the other bartenders from The Crazy Horse.

"Hey, Devon," she greets with a weird smile. "Nice baseball cap."

Shay stares daggers through her friend while I mutter, "Uh, thanks."

No idea what that means.

Shay turns to Suzie once again and asks, "Okay, what am I forgetting?"

"Nothing. You've gone over everything fifteen times. Bones and I will be fine."

"But—"

Suzie holds her hand up. "No buts. If you don't get out of here, I'm going to kick your ass."

Shay rolls her eyes. "I'd like to see you try."

I'd like to see that too.

Shay takes a seat in front of her dog and presses her forehead to his. "You be a good boy. Okay, Bones? Momma will be back in a week."

As I watch her croon to her pup, I realize I've never seen this softer side to Shay. Too bad it's toward a dog.

When she finishes her goodbyes, she stands up and grabs her giant suitcase.

"Let me help with that," I offer.

"I've got it," she defends, struggling with it the entire way out the door.

I look at Suzie. "You think she'll be that stubborn all week?"

She laughs. "Oh, I think she will be way worse than that."

I just nod and run my hand over my chin.

Suzie walks toward me. "Look, I know Shay can be a bit prickly, but I have no doubt she'll give her all in pretending to be your girlfriend this week."

"Is this where you're going to tell me to be careful? Are you going to tell me that Shay may get hurt in this whole thing?"

She laughs. "Oh, not at all. I know Shay won't let herself get hurt. That's not her. She'll put on every ounce of armor she has to prevent that. I just need you to remember there's a person underneath."

I'm not sure exactly what she means, but I know I wouldn't want to do anything to hurt Shay, so I just say, "Okay, I'll keep that in mind."

As she turns to walk away, I ask, "And you'll kick my ass if I do anything stupid?"

"Oh, sweetheart. I won't need to. Shay will kill you and make sure no one ever finds your body."

I laugh, but Suzie doesn't. Moments later, Shay walks back in. "You ready, Samson?"

"Whenever you are."

She gives Bones one final round of love before we head out the door.

When we're in the driveway, I ask, "Any regrets?"

She shakes her bangs out of her eyes. "Ask me again in a week."

Half an hour later, we are on the road and on the way to the large bed and breakfast where the wedding is being held.

We've made a little small talk but nothing too major. Shay isn't one that feels the need to constantly fill the silence even when she doesn't have anything to say. It's a nice change of pace. The only time Kyra wasn't talking was when she was mad at me.

When Shay finally does talk, she asks, "Do you think we should get our story straight?"

"Huh?" Her question catches me off-guard.

"Well, you and I are supposed to be a couple, right? What if someone asks questions about our relationship, what are we going to say?"

"Hmm. Hadn't even crossed my mind."

She looks at me with a small smirk. "Aren't you glad you brought me?"

Getting more glad by the second.

"What do you think our story should be?" I ask.

She taps the pad of her finger on the side of her cheek. "Hmm. We need to make it believable."

"How about this? I saved you from a shark attack and you fell madly in love with me during your rehabilitation process."

"Uh, I don't think so."

"Do you want to be the one who saved me from the shark?"

She puffs out a heavy sigh. "Maybe we just say we met at the bar."

"I mean, there are no sharks, but okay, I guess. Wait, that *is* how we met."

"See?" She asks. "Believable."

"If someone asks, I'll try to talk it up. I can bullshit with the best of them."

"Is that how you get all those girls to go home with you?"

"Nah, that's pure charm," I tease.

"And lots of liquor," she jokes. "Okay, let's get to know each other a little more. What's your favorite color?"

"Red. You?"

"Black."

Probably should have been obvious.

Next, she asks if I have any pets.

"Kind of."

"Devon, how do you *kind of* have a pet?"

"I kind of have a cat. She was a stray that was always hanging around. I kept feeding her and eventually let her inside to sleep. Got her a flea collar and her shots. Made sure she was fixed. She still comes and goes as she pleases, but she's sweet."

"What's her name?"

"Originally, I named her Trixie, but I thought that made her sound a little like a stripper. I didn't want other cats on the street making fun of her, so now it's Miss Trixie."

Shay just blankly looks at me, so I add, "Yes, I know it sounds insane. Just go with it."

"Alright." She draws out the word. "What kind of dog did you have with your ex?"

My heart hurts a little at the mention of the pooch. "He was a basset hound named Bruno."

She smiles. "Cute."

Good to know dogs are one thing that can crack through Shay's tough exterior.

She asks, "Speaking of your ex, is there anything I need to know before I'm forced to interact with her this week?"

"What do you mean?"

"Is she going to *warn* me about you? Or try to bring up shit that went down in your relationship?"

I think for a moment, trying to figure out how to best answer this. "Honestly, I don't know what to expect from Kyra. I would hope she's cordial. It's been almost a year, and she's dating someone new. But I also know how negative she can be. I don't know what kind of shit she could even bring up, though. She treated me like dirt for three years before finally leaving with no warning."

"She didn't give you a reason?"

I readjust the hat on my head. "Nothing more than she just wasn't happy. I really shouldn't have been surprised. We fought all the time—especially toward the end."

"I remember her coming into the bar with you once or twice. She never seemed very happy."

I start to bite one of my nails. "Yeah. The bar wasn't really her thing. Really, any place that I could have fun wasn't really her thing."

"Forgive me for asking what seem like an obvious question here, but why stay with her if she was so awful? Vagina made of gold?"

That gets a loud laugh out of me.

Shay's bold.

I like it.

"No, just a normal vagina."

"Then, what was it?"

"Fuck, Shay. I don't know. When she and I got together, it was great. We had a lot of fun. After a while, it became clear that she wanted me to be something I wasn't. I couldn't change who I was. But I think I just kept chasing that feeling we had in the beginning."

This is one of the first times I've actually talked about what happened between Kyra and myself. My brothers and friends never asked too many details, and I didn't feel like *giving* my mother those details. And the girls I've been with tend not to get too far past the small talk phase. Frankly, the only reason I'm telling Shay any of this is because she's going to have to share the same space with Kyra for a week.

Otherwise, I'd just leave it as *shit happens.*

Shay mumbles, "Yeah, I get that."

Most would think she's just being her usual sarcastic self, but I can tell from the look on her face that she really does know what I'm talking about.

"What about you?" I question. "Any serious boyfriends I should know about? Any husbands?" I joke.

"Nope. No boyfriends. And definitely no husbands."

"Ever been close?" I ask. "To getting married, I mean."

She seems to get lost in her own thoughts for a moment before finally saying, "Nope."

I feel like there's a story there, but I don't push. It's none of my business.

Even if I wanted to ask, Shay is too quick to change the topic.

"So, how do you know the bride and groom?"

"Dan and I have been best friends ever since we were in kindergarten. Even when he went off to college, we stayed close. He's had my back through it all."

"And what do you think of the bride? Think she's good enough for your boy?"

I think for a second. "I like Becky. I mean, she's not my type, but she's perfect for Dan. She can be a bit bristly, but underneath, she's a good person. I think you'll like her."

Shay gets back to asking random questions to help us get to know each other better.

I learn that her favorite food is cheeseburgers, she's obsessed with true crime and horror movies, and she plays video games when she has any free time.

Looking at her, I ask, "So, should I just seal the deal and ask you to marry me now?"

"Oh, you should be so lucky."

As we get closer to our destination, I watch her take out her piercings one by one.

"What are you doing?" I ask.

"I figure I'm supposed to be your date. I should probably look the part. I even went shopping for the occasion."

I tell her, "I didn't mean for you to go through a ton of extra trouble. You can leave your piercings in if you want."

I make a mental note to pay her back for the clothes she bought, too. After all, none of this was her idea.

"It's alright," she says. "The piercings and the clothes are easy. The tattoos are a little more difficult—at least the ones that are visible with clothes on."

Immediately my eyes look her up and down as my mind wonders where all she has tattoos that *are* hidden by clothes. I'm tempted to ask, but that would probably be rude.

Fuck, I hope I get to find out, though.

"Don't worry," I begin. "I have tattoos too. And so do the bride and groom. No one is going to ca—"

She cuts me off. "You have tattoos?"

I nod. "Well, I have *a* tattoo."

"Where?"

With a wink, I say, "I'll show you mine if you show me yours."

She gives me only what I can describe as the sexiest smile I've ever seen.

In this car ride alone, I'm started to see a whole new side of Shay. So far, I'm liking what I'm seeing. I'm not sure if that's going to make the next week easier or much, much harder.

Chapter Eight

SHAY

"Whoa. Look at this place," I say as we pull up the long, winding drive of the wedding venue.

"It's beautiful," Devon agrees.

It looks like some sort of charming old inn. Ivy grows up the walls, adding an old-timey feel to the place. Deep red rose bushes are scattered throughout the yard, off-setting all the massive trees. Squirrels scurry from one giant trunk to the next, playing a game of tag amongst themselves.

I'm guessing it's a pretty big property if the long drive is any indication.

Everything about this place screams *money.* Although I grew up on the higher end of middle class, a venue like this is way above my pay grade.

I look down at my outfit. "Should I change before we go inside? I planned on doing it before dinner, but maybe I should do it now."

"Nah, we are just going to stop by the desk and grab the key, and then, we can head straight to the room. I doubt we will see anyone along the way."

"You sure?"

He nods. "Yep. It'll be fine."

Devon pulls his large pickup truck to the front door and puts it in park. "In fact, how about I just run in real quick and make sure this is the door we need?"

"Okay, sounds good."

He gets out, and immediately, I'm bored and wish I'd gone with him. I look around at the inside of the truck; it's nice.

When he picked me up, Devon apologized for the sawdust all over the place. He said, "I tried to get it all, but I'm a carpenter. It sticks to me like glitter to a stripper."

I don't give a shit about sawdust. I'd rather have a man who works with his hands than one who sits behind a desk.

Not that I have any intention of making Devon Samson my man—although I have to say listening to him talking about his ex makes me realize that maybe there's something that runs deeper than just those good looks of his.

I get that I'm only hearing one side of the story of their breakup, but I'm tempted to believe Devon. The couple times I saw Kyra, she looked at me like I was something she stepped in. She actually looked at most people that way. This week, if she pulls that crap, I'll be quick to put her in her place. She'll learn really quickly I'm not one to be fucked with.

I about jump out of my skin when there's a tap on my window.

Looking out, I see a man with short, sandy blonde hair grinning back at me.

I guess he's thrilled he almost gave me a heart attack.

Not wanting to be rude, I roll down the window.

Still smiling, he says, "Hi. You must be Shay."

"Uhh...yeah," I reply, kind of creeped out that he already knows my name.

"I'm Dan."

"Right. The lucky groom."

His smile fades a little. "That's what she tells me."

When I have no idea how to respond to that, he adds, "Just kidding."

We stay locked in an uncomfortable silence for a moment before he says, "So, you and my boy, Devon, huh?"

Before I can answer, Devon shows back up. "Quit bugging my girl, asshat."

They both laugh and give each other a hug.

Devon says, "We'll catch up later, man. Shay and I want to decompress before dinner."

Dan gets a shit-eating grin on his face. "Oh, yeah. Decompress? Is that what they're calling it these days?"

Devon jokingly tells him to shut the fuck up and hops back in the driver's seat.

As we pull away, he looks over at me. "Sorry about that. Dan can be a bit much if you don't know him."

"He was fine. If you and I are going to pretend to be a couple, I better get used to comments like that."

He stops the truck again. "Listen. This week is supposed to be fun. If anything makes you feel uncomfortable, let me know, and I'll put an end to it."

It's a bit of an odd concept for me to hear him saying things like that. My dads taught me that men should always be respectful, but my time working in a bar has proven to me that respect is far too often overlooked. Over the years, I've learned that there are good men out there, but they seem to be a dime a dozen amongst the pigs.

Maybe Devon's one of the decent ones.

Or maybe he's just an excellent charmer.

Guess I'm about to find out.

A few minutes later, Devon and I are walking in a side door and heading to our room. The inside of this place has the same quaint charm as the outside. For the size of it, it has a very cozy and inviting feel.

It takes a few minutes to find our room, but thankfully, we don't run into anyone else along the way.

Devon sticks the small brass key into the lock. I'm surprised it's not the typical key cards you see now, but I guess they're trying to adhere to a certain theme.

Everything is reminiscent of an old Victorian style house with the deep, beautiful colors and dark, ornate wood.

He swings open the heavy mahogany door and gestures for me to enter first.

That theme I was talking about? It's even more present in here. Cream-colored carpet covers the floors, and the walls are painted a dark red. The wood of the dresser, end tables, and bed are all a pretty cherry color.

Speaking of beds, there's just one of them.

As if able to read my mind, Devon says, "Don't worry. I can take the couch."

"Not necessary," I tell him. "It's plenty big enough for the both of us."

"Okay, that shower is amazing," I say, walking out in a fluffy bathrobe.

Devon sits on the bed, flipping aimlessly through the channels. "Well, put it right up there with the TV. This thing has 400 channels."

"Are there even 400 different things to watch?"

"Nope."

"Shower's all yours," I tell him, and he turns off the TV.

Since getting in here, things have been a little awkward. I'm not sure why other than the fact that both of us are a little nervous of the parts we are about to play.

Some nerves never hurt anyone, though. They've always kept me going.

I open my suitcase and try to figure out what to wear tonight. Devon said this dinner wasn't too formal, but I still want to make a good first impression. Otherwise, no one is going to buy what we're selling. This thing needs to look believable.

I pull out one of the black dresses that I bought and hold it up. This one will do, I guess. I also grab a bra and a pair of peep toe heels that I bought the other day.

As I search through my suitcase, I quickly realize something's missing.

Underwear.

I forgot underwear.

I bought all new sexy ones, and I left them all sitting in my washing machine.

"No, no, no!" I mutter as I frantically search as though some might magically appear. I could probably just go buy more—if we weren't in the middle of Bum Fuck Egypt.

I guess I'm going panty-less...for now anyway.

Over the next twenty minutes, I get dressed and do my hair and makeup. It's not my normal style, but I don't think I look half bad.

I just hope Devon agrees. The look he gives me when he comes out of the bathroom tells me I'm safe.

"Damn, Shay," he says with his mouth hanging open.

"Do I look alright?"

"You look incredible."

"Good enough to play your girlfriend?" I ask.

He walks my direction and only stops when he's right in front of me. I can smell whatever good smelling soap he used. It smells like cedar or sandalwood or something—one of those woodsy smells that likely has a weird name like "dragon's breath".

His blue eyes stare down at me. "If I got to call you my girlfriend, I'd consider myself one lucky son of a bitch."

I shoot him a sly smile. "Guess maybe you should go buy a lottery ticket then."

Chapter Nine

DEVON

When I come out of the bathroom, I had no idea I'd find Shay standing there looking fucking stunning. Mind you, Shay's always a looker.

But I had no fucking clue what she was hiding under those jeans and baggy shirts. Curvy is a damn understatement.

I feel like a pervert because I can't seem to stop staring at her ample chest. What is normally hidden under rock band t-shirts is now pushed up and on full display.

Stop staring.

Stop staring.

The short dress she's wearing also shows off her juicy hips and thick thighs.

My eyes spot a tattoo on her right foot and follow it all the way up the entire side of her body. Dark green vines wind up and down with flowers and other images scattered throughout. I've always been able to see the part that's on her arm, but I had no idea that it spanned so much of her body.

Realizing I'm still staring at her like she's a piece of meat, and I'm a hungry wolf, I reluctantly pull my eyes back to look at her face. Even her makeup is different. Her usual dark eyeshadow has been replaced. She still has a smokey eye, but it's a lot lighter than normal. The color she has paired with it makes her eyes really pop.

"Devon, you okay?" She pulls me from my thoughts.

"Yeah, sorry. Just trying to take it all in."

She pokes her finger into my chest. "Don't get used to it. This week is a one-time thing."

She goes to walk away, but I grab her by the hand and pull her back.

"What are you doing?" She asks.

"Well, you're supposed to be my girlfriend, right?"

She nods, her eyes never leaving mine.

"Then, I think I should tell you that I don't care what you wear or what makeup you have on, you still look damn fine."

I swear I see something soften in her eyes, but I figure I must be imagining it when she says, "Man, you're good."

Instead of telling her that I'm actually completely serious, I decide to just play it off like a joke. "Oh yeah, you like that?"

Looking down, I realize she hasn't let go of my hand yet. Our fingers are still locked together.

My eyes move back to hers, as I try to figure out what she's thinking. She doesn't make me wonder long, though.

"May as well get used to holding hands, right?" She asks.

"Guess so."

I'm tempted to kiss her to break any lingering tension between the two of us. But I don't want to push it.

She's the first to break our intense stare, looking toward the clock. "Should we get going?"

"Probably."

We take a moment to make sure we have everything we need. As we're walking out the door, she turns around to look at me.

"For what it's worth, you look nice, too. Really nice."

"Thank you."

She stops. "Oh, I need to tell you something before we go. It may not be the best time, but—"

"What is it, Shay?"

She swallows the lump in her throat. "I sort of...forgot...my underwear."

It takes me a moment to process what she's saying. "You forgot your..."

"Underwear. Aside from the pair I had on when we got here."

"Umm. How?"

She groans. "I bought some new ones and washed them because otherwise...gross. And I forgot about them in the washing machine."

Unable to hide my smile, I ask, "So, you're just going to walk around with no panties?"

"Apparently. But since most of what I brought are all dresses, I need you to keep me on my toes and make sure I don't flash anyone a glimpse of my naughty bits."

"How should I do that?"

She uses her hands as she speaks. "Look, I'm not always the most ladylike when I sit. Just make sure I'm not sitting with my legs wide open or something."

Wiggling my eyebrows at her, I ask, "What if I *want* to catch a glimpse of your lady bits?"

Shay punches me in the shoulder. "Devon!"

"Alright, alright. I'll make sure no one sees anything they shouldn't."

"Thank you."

She spins around in a circle, running her hands over the bottom of the dress. "Can you tell I'm not wearing any?"

"No," I answer honestly.

But I know she's not wearing any. And my cock knows it too.

And neither of us will be able to stop thinking about it all fucking night.

When we walk onto the large patio area where a long table is set up for dinner, I see that we are two of the last people to show up. I take Shay's hand in mine, ready for whatever is to come. Everyone stops talking and turns to look at us.

"Sorry, I didn't think we were late," I say.

Dan smiles. "You're not. Glad you two made it."

As everyone continues to look at us, I squeeze Shay's hand, letting her know I've got her back.

We make our way to two of the empty seats at the end of the table.

Dan speaks to everyone. "This is my best friend, Devon, and his girlfriend, Shay."

Everybody mutters hello while Becky scoffs at the word *girlfriend.* My eyes flick over to Kyra who is staring daggers through the both of us. Thankfully, the table is big enough that we are nowhere near her or her boyfriend—who looks like he just stepped out of a GQ magazine with his perfectly quaffed hair and manicured nails.

If that's what she was after, I see why she moved on from me. Looking at her face, I think she looks as unhappy as ever. But I'm starting to think that's what her face always looks like. Now that we're not together, I wonder exactly what I saw in her. Right now, the look on her face like she smells something foul isn't the most attractive.

I pull the chair out for Shay and then take a seat next to her.

"You okay?" I lean in to whisper.

"I'm good. I'm a goth girl, Devon. Weird looks and stares come with the territory."

We aren't sitting very close to the bride and groom, so I hope we can avoid some of the inevitable questions that will be launched our way.

A waiter appears and asks what we would like to drink. I order a beer, and Shay asks for tequila.

Confused, the waiter asks, "Tequila with?'

Shay makes eye contact with him. "More tequila."

I ask, "Straight to the point, huh?"

"I'm not sure any other way to do it."

A redheaded woman across from us introduces herself. "Hi, I'm Shelly. I went to college with the bride."

"Nice to meet you, Shelly. I'm Devon. I've known the groom since we were five, and this is my girlfriend, Shay."

She smiles and makes a little small talk about how beautiful the venue is.

Looking around at all the freshly cut flowers and twinkle lights draped everywhere, I have to agree.

Shelly squints her eyes and stares at Shay. "You look so familiar. Do I know you from somewhere?"

Shay thinks for a moment and replies, "I don't think so."

But Shelly's not convinced. She taps her finger on her chin. "I swear I know you."

Seeing Shay looking very uncomfortable, I opt to change the subject. "So, Shelly, are you here alone?"

"For now. My husband, Al, isn't able to come up until later in the week."

Thankfully, someone a couple seats down gets Shelly's attention, and our drinks show up.

"Thank God," Shay mumbles.

I whisper, "Sorry. No idea what was up with her."

"It's alright," she replies, downing half of the tequila.

I have a feeling I'll be apologizing quite a bit this week.

It isn't long before the food starts being served, one course at a time. There's a soup to start with followed by a salad, a shrimp cocktail, a steak, and a chocolate mousse for dessert. It's all delicious, but the best part is that no one else really talks to us the rest of the meal. Instead, Shay asks me questions about everyone else that sits around the giant table.

I point out the ones I actually know. One is Dan's little sister, Wendy, who is an exotic dancer outside of Dallas.

Shay asks, "And I'm the one getting dirty looks?"

"Well, aside from Dan, no one else knows."

Shay gives me some side eye. "And you."

"Dan can't keep a secret from me to save his life. But everyone else in their family thinks she's still in med school."

Shay gasps. "How scandalous!"

"Oh, just wait until you hear about the dirt on Becky's parent. You'll see them at the actual wedding I assume."

Her eyes go wide. "Tell me."

"Well, her dad is a stockbroker and has an affinity for working girls. Her mom refuses to leave because there's an ironclad prenup in place, so she started sleeping with her tennis pro to get back at him."

Sarcastically, Shay says, "How romantic. And everyone knows and just pretends it isn't happening? Even Becky?"

The waiter brings over another round of drinks, and I take a sip of beer before replying. "It's been going on for years. Everyone's used to it. I think Becky uses it for leverage to get what she wants—like a big, fancy wedding."

She laughs. "Rich people are wild."

Much to my dismay, Becky comes walking over to us. It's like Beetlejuice—say her name enough, and she'll appear.

Realizing what's about to happen, Shay sets her hand on my thigh to try to sell this whole thing. I'm sure it's unintentional, but she's close enough to my cock to have it threatening to stretch my pants.

Now is not the fucking time.

In a snarky tone, Becky greets, "Hey, you two lovebirds."

"Hi, Becky," I say.

Shay holds out her hand. "Nice to meet you, Becky. I'm Shay."

The look Becky gives shows she's trying to make her determinations about Shay, but she shakes her hand anyway.

Becky points between the two of us. "So, how did you two meet?" She crosses her arms over her chest like she's sure she has us beat.

Shay answers, "I'm actually a bartender, and Devon came into my bar a lot."

Becky's lips purse together. "I'm sure he did."

I decide to take it from here. "I got stood up on a date, and I went in to grab a drink. Shay took pity on me and bought me a beer. We shut the bar down that night, talking and getting to know each other better."

While I talk, Shay leans back against my chest, so I set my hands on her hips. "It was like for the first time, I was able to see how amazing Shay was. You ever heard the saying *sometimes you can't see what's right in front of you?*"

Shay leans back to give me a soft kiss on the cheek. "We've been inseparable ever since."

"Mm-hmm," Becky mumbles, clearly not convinced.

Thankfully, Dan interrupts. "Come on, beautiful. Let's go dance."

"Now?" she asks.

"Yes, now. There's a dance floor, and we paid for a DJ all damn week. I'm going to dance every chance I get."

That gets Becky to smile and follow her fiancé to the floor. The DJ turns on a slow song, and the two of them start to sway.

I lean close to whisper to Shay, "You did great."

"Our audience isn't quite done yet. Your ex is staring."

Of course, she is.

I try to ignore it, but it's beyond uncomfortable. "Sorry," I tell her.

A few other couples get up to join in on the dance floor. To try to escape Kyra, I ask, "Do you want to dance?"

I expect her to tell me to fuck off, but she doesn't. She takes my hand and lets me lead her to the floor. I pull her close, holding one hand in mine and holding her hip with the other.

We stumble for a moment before I ask, "Are you going to let me lead?"

"My bad," she says with a hint of embarrassment.

Soon enough, we are in a nice rhythm, moving with the beat of the music.

"Devon," Shay whispers.

"Yes, dear?" I joke.

"I feel like everyone's staring."

Because they are.

Since I don't want her to take any of this too seriously, I say in a low voice, "They can probably tell you're not wearing any underwear."

She slaps me on the shoulder but laughs. "Shut up."

"We could really give them something to talk about and have you go braless."

"Oh, now, Devon, we don't want anyone to lose an eye with these giant things swinging around."

"Speaking of which, this may sound awful, but where the hell have you been hiding those things?"

To my surprise, she throws her head back and laughs. "Yeah, I tend to keep them under lockdown."

"Why?"

"I'm a bartender, and men are pigs."

"Got it. Say no more." I watched my mom date every asshole in the state of Texas. I know how some of them can be. I imagine it's worse in a bar where there's alcohol involved.

As we turn, I see everyone really is staring at us. "Do you think they're onto us?"

She doesn't answer but says, "Kiss me."

"What?"

Her eyes look into mine. "You heard me, Cassanova. Kiss me."

Chapter Ten

SHAY

Devon stares down at me as I wait for him to make his move. The truth is I've been wanting to stick it to his ex all night. She won't quit staring at me, and I'm ready to give her something to look at.

Devon pulls me closer so that my body is pressed firmly against his. Man, he smells good.

Leaning down, he softly presses his lips against mine. It's a little awkward with people watching us, and we stumble a little through it. Nerves seem to be getting the best of us.

When he pulls back to look at me, I say, "I think we can do better than that."

Grabbing him by the collar of his shirt, I pull him to me. This time, I open for him, letting his tongue slip inside. It expertly dances with mine, and I realize that if he's this good at kissing, the rumors about him eating pussy are probably true.

Do I want to find out?

Maybe.

But one step at a time.

I'm not sure if it's the way he kisses, or the excitement that we are being watched, but my heart flutters in my chest.

We stand there kissing long enough to make it look believable but not long enough to make it weird. When we pull apart, we go back to dancing until my poor feet can't take anymore.

"Can we go sit down?" I ask. "These shoes are killing me."

"Of course."

Once we get back to our seats, the waiter brings us another round.

"This is a magical place," I say. "Alcohol just appears."

Devon turns toward me and pats his lap. "Give me your feet."

"Why?"

"You said they hurt. I'll rub them."

I honestly can't believe Devon is being so accommodating on this trip. Sure, I know I'm doing him a favor, but he's been quick to make sure I'm happy and comfortable. It's crazy that my pretend boyfriend treats me better than most of my actual ones have.

Maybe that's the trick—keep all your boyfriends pretend.

I kick off my heels and prop my feet up in his lap, careful not to flash my naughty bits in the process.

When he starts rubbing, my head falls back, and I let out a moan. Immediately, I look up to see if anyone heard, but it looks like we are in the clear.

Devon heard me, though, because he says, "You can't do that—especially when I know you don't have any panties on."

"Why?" I ask coyly. "What are you thinking about?"

"Oh, you don't want to know."

"Try me."

But before he can, Kyra walks up beside us. "Hi, Devon."

She glances at me but otherwise ignores my presence.

"Hi, Kyra. What do you want?" He asks, annoyed.

"Why do I have to want something? Can't I just say hi?" The sound of her voice reminds me of nails on a chalkboard.

Before Devon can answer, my smart mouth jumps into action. "Sure, you can say hi—as long as you're saying bye in the same sentence."

She shoots me one of those dirtiest looks I've ever seen. She says, "Wow, Devon's really scraping the bottom of the barrel with you."

"You say that, yet you can't seem to take your eyes off me," I quip.

Before she can retort, I grab Devon by the hand and stand up. "Come on, baby. Let's head back to the room and have some *alone* time. That way, Kyra can watch us walk away."

I hold my heels in one hand and hold Devon's hand with the other as we leave the patio.

Leaning close, Devon whispers, "That may be the sexiest thing I've ever seen."

"Considering this is only night one, you'll probably see a lot more of that this week."

Without even looking at him, I can tell he's smiling. "I can't fucking wait."

I'm happy to get away from everyone else, and we've almost made a clean getaway.

But Becky stops us before we get too far. "You two heading out?"

Devon answers, "Yeah. We just wanted to have some alone time."

She licks her tongue over her teeth. "Mm-hmm."

"But dinner was great."

She takes another step closer to us and says, "I'm not sure if you two have Daniel snowed, but I'm not buying it. I saw that kiss. No sparks. It looked like that was your first-time locking lips with each other. You're going to have to do a lot more convincing than that."

Before either of us can argue against her claims, she walks away.

And the two of us hurry back to our room, hoping not to have any more encounters along the way.

When we are safely inside, we stop and look at each other, not saying a word until both of us burst out laughing. I have no idea what's so funny, but we have a case of the giggles. I feel like we're a couple of kids who just escaped a lecture from our parents. Every time we start to quiet down, we look at each other and start all over again.

When we finally get it all out of our systems, I say, "Man, that Becky is a tough cookie."

"No joke. And with this whole thing, she'll be a dog with a fucking bone."

"I can't believe she didn't believe our kiss," I say. "I thought it was pretty believable."

"Hell, yeah, it was." He moves so that his large frame is standing directly in front of me. "I guess next time we will just need to be more convincing."

As I stare up into his blue eyes, I feel like I'm being hypnotized. I see why so many women fall into bed with him.

Well, that and his devilish good looks.

And his immense charm.

I never thought I'd consider being another notch on Devon Samson's bedpost but here I am—considering it. Despite what Becky may have thought, our kiss was full of fireworks. I want to do it more.

Moving an inch closer, I say, "Maybe we should practice. You know, to help make it more believable."

With a small smile, he says, "Makes perfect sense."

Setting one hand on the small of my back, he pulls me in so that I'm pressed against him. His other hand grabs the side of my face. As he moves his lips to mine, he says, "And this time, I can really do it right."

Before I can think about his words, he kisses me. It's the kind of kiss that makes me want to bring down every wall I've ever built around myself—if that's even possible.

It makes my head go fuzzy, taking away my ability to think about anything besides Devon. My entire body melts against him as his tongue slips in and out of my mouth.

Just when I start to get lost in the moment, he pulls back. "How was that?"

I run my finger over my bottom lip. "Definitely better. But I still don't know if Becky will believe it. Maybe we should try again just to be sure."

"You're probably right." This time, he grabs my face with both hands and kisses me with even more passion than before.

If there was ever an instruction manual written on how to kiss, Devon Samson should author it. If he keeps doing this, I'm likely to forget my own name.

It's incredible.

But I want more.

This time, I'm the one to pull back. Breathless, I say, "You know what I think might help?"

He raises his eyebrows, waiting for my answer.

"Maybe we need to get more comfortable with each other. Keep going and see what happens. Hard to deny our chemistry if we've done more than kiss."

He thinks for a moment. "Do you mean something like this?"

Without wasting another moment, his hands reach below my ass and lift me so that my legs wrap around his waist. His mouth gets back to work kissing me.

Between kisses, I say, "Yeah, just like this."

His hands hold onto my thighs, but I silently beg for them to move up to grab my ass. Really, I want those big hands of his anywhere and everywhere.

"What about this?" He asks.

He holds onto me with one hand while using the other to tangle his fingers in my hair. He pulls my head back, exposing my neck for him to kiss and bite.

"Mm-hmm." I moan.

If I were wearing panties right now, they'd be soaked.

"Devon," I whisper.

"Yes, Shay?" He asks, still kissing.

"Take my dress off."

That gets him to stop and look at me. "Are you sure? We don't have to do anything if you don't want to."

I stop him. "Devon, I said take my dress off."

That's all the convincing he needs. He walks us to the bed, setting me on my feet before sitting on the edge of the mattress.

Looking into my eyes, he says, "You want me to stop, and I do. No questions asked."

I nod. But as much as I appreciate the respect thing, I have no intentions of telling him to stop. I've been thinking about this all evening. We're both single but are supposed to be pretending to be a couple. Why not *act* like a couple?

As Devon's fingers reach around the back of my neck to undo the zipper of the dress, he starts to speak.

"Do you know how difficult it's been, trying not to get hard while thinking about you not wearing panties all night?"

I give him a sexy smile. "Now, you don't have to try anymore."

Grabbing my hand, he yanks it down until it's firmly touching the bulge in his pants. "Sunshine, my cock couldn't go down right now even if I wanted it to."

Devon's little nickname for me to mock my less-than-cherry disposition suddenly feels much more serious now when he's dirty talking and getting me naked.

But I know things with Devon *aren't* serious. This whole thing is just an act.

And there's something hot about him having a little pet name for me—almost as hot as his dirty talk.

Almost.

His fingers grip the top of my zipper and slowly pull it down until he's able to drag the dress down my body. When it falls to the floor, I stand before him in nothing more than my bra.

I'm not the skinniest girl in the world. I have a poochy stomach, thick thighs, and wide hips. My boobs hang a little low, and my ass is sometimes too big for my pants. But I've learned to love all those things. I've embraced my body, and my philosophy is that any man who doesn't like it, doesn't deserve to go to bed with me.

The look on Devon's face, though, shows that he does like it.

A lot.

"Holy shit, Shay. You mean to tell me this is what you've been hiding under those jeans and t-shirts?"

"I like keeping some mystery," I say with a small laugh.

His hands move onto my bra, which he unhooks and lets it fall in a heap with the dress.

Devon takes a look at the small barbells through my pierced nipples and looks up at me. "You really are a mystery."

He grabs my hips, urging me to take a step closer to him. I do, and his mouth closes around one of my nipples. He gently sucks, causing the metal to pull slightly and send sparks of electricity straight to my pussy. His tongue swirls around the tip while I let out a loud moan.

He moves to the other one and does the same. It feels incredible but is also driving me crazy. Patience has never been a virtue of mine.

With my hands on his shoulders, I push him so that he's flat on his back. Climbing on top of him, I kiss him before pulling his shirt off over his head. In the dim glow of the bedside lamp, I see the tattoo he was talking about. On one side of his chest, he has a large lion's head done all in black ink. It's beautiful.

He's beautiful with his broad chest and hard stomach. There's no six pack, but he's fit from doing physical work all day every day.

His rough hands rub softly over my skin as I start at his neck, working my way down his chest and stomach, leaving soft bites along the way. I feel his muscles tense underneath my touch as I get closer to his dick.

When I finally reach the button of his jeans, I waste no time in pulling them from his body. Then, come the boxers. When his cock is finally free, I see that it's beautiful too.

Good lord.

It's not the longest I've been with, but it's certainly the thickest—by a wide margin. A throbbing vein runs along the underside, leading to the large head.

I run my tongue from his balls all the way to the tip, prompting a guttural groan from Devon. I suck the head into my mouth, taking him as far down my throat as I can.

"Motherfucker, Shay," he hisses. "That feels amazing."

If I had my tongue ring in, it'd feel even better.

"Do you have condoms?" I ask.

"In my suitcase."

Of course, he does. He's Devon Samson.

I get up off of him to go try to find them, but before I can comprehend what's happening, he pulls me back until I'm flat on my back on the bed with him on top of me.

Whispering in my ear, he says, "I know you're impatient, Sunshine, but I'm not nearly done with you yet." Moving down my body, he adds, "Spread your legs, Shay. Let me see this pussy."

My knees fall open, completely exposing myself to him.

He sees my hood piercing in my clit and says, "You're really trying to kill me, aren't you? Do you have any idea how sexy you are?"

"Show me," I taunt.

"My pleasure."

His tongue slowly moves to lick the curved barbell that runs vertically through the hood of my clit. I'm so turned on that my sensitivity is heightened already, but the piercing makes it even more so.

Using his teeth, he gently tugs on it, causing my back to arch off the bed. He teases only a moment more before really getting down to business.

It takes mere seconds to realize why women call Devon Mr. Pussy. The man seems to be perfectly in tune with my vagina, knowing exactly what I like and doing it over and over again.

You know when you get a new vibrator, and you cycle through all the settings until you inevitably land on your *favorite* one? Devon's tongue tries a plethora of different tricks and techniques until pinpointing exactly what I like and then sticking with it.

Oh, yeah. I get it now.

My fingertips grip the sheets as my entire body writhes on the bed. Devon hooks his arms around my thighs to hold me in place while he finishes his heavenly work.

"Oh, fuck," I moan. "Right there! Don't fucking move!"

Most men hear those words and immediately decide to change it up, but not Devon. He keeps doing exactly the same thing—I'm not even sure what to call it because honestly, it feels like the man has two tongues.

Seconds later, my entire body convulses as I practically scream through my orgasm. Devon keeps licking, careful not to stop until he's sure I've come every drop.

When my pussy is too sensitive to take anymore, he sits up, looking at me with a cocky grin on his face.

Oh, he knows exactly what he's doing.

Why is that so hot?

But as great as the pussy eating was, I'm ready to find out what other tricks Devon has up his sleeve.

Chapter Eleven

DEVON

L ook, I've been with a lot of women in my life—most of them in the past year. I love them in every shape, every size. Long hair, short hair, light, or dark, it doesn't matter. I love them all.

But Shay Baxter?

Holy hell, she's a whole other breed.

Is it her piercings?

Her tattoos?

Her curves?

Sure, all those things are sexy as fuck, and I don't know that I'll be able to get enough of them. But what really makes Shay one of the sexiest women I've ever been with is her confidence. She's hot, and she knows it.

If I wasn't so anxious to fuck her, I would have eaten her pussy all night long, making her come again and again. But I *need* to know what it feels like to bury myself inside her.

I don't know that I've ever needed anything more.

I look down at her while I roll the condom on over my dick. I stop to just stare for a moment. I don't want to forget what she looks like right now. Her hair is messily fanned out under her head, and her curves are on full display. Her tongue licks over her bottom lip as her pretty eyes stare back at me.

Spreading her thighs, she moves her hand between them. "Come on, Cassanova. Are you going to fuck me, or should I take matters into my own hands?"

Lord, this woman is going to be the death of me.

I grab her hand and move it out of the way. "Buckle up, Sunshine."

In one quick thrust, I push inside her. We both release a simultaneous moan as her pussy stretches to fit around me. It's just as good as I thought it was going to be.

No, scratch that.

It's better.

She matches every move I make. If I go harder and faster, her hips move in perfect rhythm with me. Her back arches so she can get close enough to me for her to kiss and bite my neck.

She hooks her ankles around my waist, pulling me even deeper into her while her nails claw at my back.

"Harder," she moans. "Fuck me harder, Devon."

I do as she asks, my hips pounding into her with every thrust. Usually, I'd worry if was going too hard—I never want anything to hurt. But Shay is a fucking animal, craving it as hard and as fast as I can give it to her.

I drop my head down to take one of her nipple rings between my teeth while my tongue licks the sensitive flesh around it. Her hands fist in my hair, holding me in place, letting me know how much she likes it.

If I had any idea what I was missing, I would have tried to take Shay home ages ago. But I had no clue. She's like a sexy little package, ready to explode and get wild the moment you unwrap her.

"Fuck, girl," I hiss, trying to keep ahold of any little bit of control I may still have. "That pussy feels so good."

She gives a loud moan in response.

"You want to come on this cock?"

"Mm-hmm."

Leaning back to sit on my knees, I keep fucking her hard like she asked but also use the pad of my thumb to start rubbing circles around her clit. I do it just hard enough to apply some pressure to her piercing but not enough to make anything painful.

She shifts her hips and says, "Up just a little."

Fuck, I love when a woman isn't afraid to ask for what she wants.

Once I hit the right spot, she cries, "Don't stop. Right there. Don't you fucking move!"

I wouldn't dream of it, Sunshine.

Her pussy clenches around me, squeezing tighter the closer she gets. It feels so good I don't know how much longer I'm going to last. Her vice grip is going to have me coming sooner rather than later.

It takes less than a minute for her body to start bucking off the bed as she rides out her orgasm. Watching her come is everything. She's fucking perfect. Her chest glistens with a thin sheen while her cheeks blush the softest shade of pink. Her back arches, and her hands try to grab onto anything that's within reach.

Between the sight of it, and the way her pussy grips me for dear life, I can't hold on any longer. I pound into her with a few more hard strokes before filling the condom.

I lean down to give her one more kiss before pulling out.

When I get back from throwing the condom in the trash, she's still lying naked, sprawled out on the bed.

Breathless, she says, "Holy shit."

"You aren't kidding," I agree. "I don't think anyone can say shit about our chemistry now."

I disappear into the bathroom for a minute, and when I get back, I see Shay making a wall of pillows down the center of the bed.

"Uh, Shay...what are you doing?"

"Building a wall. There will be no cuddling."

"Can I ask why?"

She looks at me. "It's too personal."

Chuckling, I reply, "You just came on my face and my cock. That's not too personal?"

"No, that's sex," she replies with a matter-of-fact attitude. "Sex is fun. Sex is able to be had with no strings attached. Cuddling is for people who want the strings. I'm not one of them. We can use this bed for sleeping or sex. That's it."

The way she talks about it makes me think that some asshole has left her jaded along the way, but I don't dare ruin the evening we just had by asking about it. This is our first night here. Maybe throughout the week, I can get a few more glimpses into the world of Shay Baxter.

Until then, I'll be happy just sleeping next to her.

Pillow wall or not.

Chapter Twelve

SHAY

"So, you're telling me that we're just spending an entire day at the pool?" I ask Devon.

"Apparently. Why is that weird?"

"I guess it just seems like an odd way to spend a whole day so close to a wedding."

While wearing nothing but a towel around his waist, he searches through his suitcase. "Hey, this is one of the only times this week I get to wear my baseball hat. I'll take it. And I think they're just trying to do something fun to loosen everyone up. Kind of break the ice, you know?"

"I guess."

"What's wrong? You don't like swimming?"

"Haven't done it much in a pool. I'm more of a lake gal. I haven't been in a pool in years."

"Really?"

My face scrunches up. "People pee in pools."

He rubs the stubble on his chin. "People pee in lakes, too."

"Lakes are bigger. Less of a pee to water ratio."

His eyes look at the ceiling as though thinking over what I just said. "Hate to tell you this, Sunshine, but pee is pee."

"You're not making the pool seem any more appealing." I laugh.

I reposition on the bed, trying to get motivated to get up and put my bathing suit on. These soft, pillowy sheets don't want to release their grip on me.

I watch Devon yank the towel off his waist and set it on the bed. There, staring back at me is his thick boxer beast. That thing is just as skillful as his mouth.

Who knew that was even possible?

Even soft, Devon's cock is a thing of beauty.

Last night, while he was fucking me like there was no tomorrow, I came to one very important conclusion.

This week, I'm going to get as much of that good dick as I can. I figure when we leave this place and head home, we'll go right back to the way things were. Heaven knows I'm not looking for any type of relationship, and I'm sure Mr. Pussy will want to go back to spreading his seed all over town.

But while we're here, playing pretend for a week, why not make the most of it? Devon Samson's cock is a terrible thing to waste. I now know that from firsthand experience.

I'm honestly surprised that a woman hasn't already tried to lock him down. Maybe he doesn't want that. Or maybe they know once you catch the white whale, it would be selfish to keep it to yourself and not share it with the rest of the world.

I don't intend on keeping him—I don't keep anyone anymore—but this week, he's mine.

Well, kind of.

Close enough.

Devon gets my attention. "Are you okay? What's going on in that noggin of yours?"

"Just wishing we could stay here in this nice comfortable bed all day," I respond with a slight pout.

"Still tired?" He asks, slipping his trunks on, covering up the beast.

I might assume he doesn't know what I'm actually hinting at...until he gives me a devilish wink.

Man, that's so freaking sexy.

Positioning his arms on the bed, he leans toward me until he's close enough to kiss me. But his lips don't touch mine.

Instead, he whispers, "How about we make it through this day, and then, when we get back, I'll make you come as many times as you can handle?"

"Can't we just skip to that part?" I tease.

"Nope. I have to reward you somehow."

"Would showing you my boobs make any difference?"

"Hell, I'm never going to say no to seeing them, but we still have to go to the pool. Believe me, I'd much rather stay in here with you."

A small twinge of guilt hits me because the wedding stuff is the whole reason we came here, and I'm complaining about it. I sound like a brat.

"Sorry," I say. "Of course, we're going. Just let me shave my legs real quick, and we can get out of here."

I stand up and head for the shower. Before I can get very far, Devon grabs my arm, spinning me around to face him. His fingers lightly trace the outline of my jaw.

"I really would rather stay in here with you. You know that, right?"

I nod my head.

"You believe me?"

Normally, I'd think he was just another man, completely full of shit.

But strangely enough, I *do* believe him.

What the hell is up with that?

As we walk into the pool area, I say, "If Kyra wouldn't quit staring last night, I can only imagine what she will be like with me in a bathing suit."

"Let her stare," Devon says.

"Oh, she can eat her heart out. I don't give a fuck where she looks."

"She's probably envious of your tits. She always hated her small ones."

"Hmm. That makes me feel better."

He grins. "Glad I could help."

Dan walks over to greet us, wearing a Hawaiian shirt and matching trunks. "Morning, lovebirds."

"Morning," we greet in unison.

Devon takes my hand in his, trying to sell this thing a little more.

Dan points to a table under a large cabana. "There's brunch over there. Bagels, fruit, mimosas—the works. Feel free to dig in whenever you're ready."

I'm ready now. Multiple orgasms really works up an appetite.

We walk over to the table and take a seat. Once again, we are the last to arrive and are forced to sit in closer proximity to Kyra than I'd like. Already, she's glaring at me.

Oh well. Guess I'll just have to give her something to stare at.

As we fill up our plates, I look around the table. There are a few more people that seemed to have trickled in between last night and now.

A waiter comes around with a tray of mimosas. Champaigne isn't really my thing, but I'm guessing there's no tequila at brunch. Deciding to take what I can get, I grab a glass off the tray, and Devon follows suit.

Just when I'm about to take a bite of the bagel I smothered in cream cheese, Dan stands up to talk.

Oh, come on. I'm so hungry.

He clinks his knife on the side of the flute to get everyone's attention.

"Good morning, everyone. Thanks for coming out this morning. We just wanted to have some fun today and let everyone get to know each other before the big day. We're only missing a couple more that will show up later in the week. Anyway, I hope everyone has a good time. Food will be restocked all afternoon, and the bar will open a little later on. Love all of you." He raises his glass, and the rest of us cheers each other.

I catch Kyra giving me a dirty look, and I sigh under my breath. Looking back at her, I ask, "You okay, Kyra? You don't look so hot. Feeling alright?"

"Oh, I'm fine," she retorts. "Just thinking how nice it must be to not have to worry about eating carbs. I could never eat a bagel like *that* if I want to stay looking like *this.*"

"Yeah, I love bagels," I say, biting off a huge chunk. With a mouthful, I add, "Luckily for me, most of the carbs I eat go straight to my tits. Guess you don't have *that* problem."

Devon chokes on the swig of his mimosa he just took. He covers his mouth to stifle his laugh.

I can see Kyra grinding her teeth, but thankfully, it keeps her mouth shut.

For now.

Devon leans closer to me. He whispers low enough for just us to hear. "Okay, I was wrong last night. *That* was the hottest thing I've ever seen."

"Glad you liked it."

We get on with our meal without further issue. In fact, I don't pay much attention to Kyra at all, but a heated exchange between her and her boyfriend gets my attention.

Mr. Perfect Hair and Nails gets a phone call. He's already been texting the whole time, and now, he has no qualms with how his phone may be disturbing everyone else. He stands up to answer, but Kyra grabs his arm.

"Baby, do you really have to answer? Can't you just put the phone away?" She doesn't ask in her typical bitchy tone. This one is much more sincere.

Snapping his head to look back at her, the man barks, "Don't start with me, Kyra. You're lucky I'm here at all. I'll be right back."

Her face falls as her boyfriend breaks free of her grip and walks away. I hear him answer with, "Hey, you."

His tone suggests the call is from someone other than a coworker or even a friend, but I guess I don't know that for sure.

I stare at Kyra, seeing a crack in her armor and a glimpse of her vulnerability underneath. I've been where she is—with a man who kept his secrets. One who looked great on paper but was an actual narcissist. And I'd get that same look on my face that Kyra wears now.

When she notices me staring, her entire demeanor changes. The cold hard bitch is back in play. It's hard to feel sorry for someone who looks at you like you're a bug she wants to squash.

Yet somehow, I still do.

Glaring at me, she asks, "Something you want to say? Chad had to take a work call." *Of course her boyfriend's name is Chad.* "Some people have real jobs that are more important than slinging drinks all night."

Alright, the feeling has passed.

Chapter Thirteen

DEVON

You know how a lot of women go to the pool and don't want to get their hair wet or just want to sunbathe all day?

That's not Shay.

Not even a little bit.

For a woman who doesn't like pools, she sure looks like she's having the time of her life. She played on all the floats before challenging me to a swordfight with pool noodles.

Seeing how much fun Shay was having convinced others to get in the pool instead of just watching. Kyra seems to have disappeared with her new Prince Charming, which I'm more than thankful for. I half expect her and Shay to come to blows by the end of the week. As much as I'd love to see Shay beat Kyra's ass in a girl fight, I think the bride may frown upon it.

Shay moves around, bouncing up and down on a pool noodle with a pair of goggles sitting on top of her head.

Not able to contain my smile, I say, "You know for someone who thinks pools are gross, you seem to be enjoying yourself."

"Eh, when in Rome, I guess. Besides, there aren't really any kids here. Aren't they the ones who usually pee in pools?"

I resist the urge to tell her that I'm sure it's not *just* kids. She's having way too much fun to ruin it for her.

Pulling the goggles down over her eyes, she says, "Let's play mermaids."

I have no idea what that means, but before I can ask, she dives under the surface and swims away.

Never in my wildest dreams did I think Shay Baxter would be playing mermaids in a swimming pool. The tough-as-nails goth chick is having the best time.

And it's fucking adorable.

Hell, I think this is the first time I've seen Shay without the heavy eye makeup and eyeliner.

I think she's beautiful either way. Makeup's never been a big deal to me one way or another.

Deciding to play along with her, I toss my hat on one of the chairs so that I can go under the water and follow her to the other side of the pool, careful to avoid the legs of anyone wading around the edges. I open my eyes under the water, but even with everything blurry, Shay's sexy tattooed legs are unmistakable.

When she's flat on her feet, I wrap my arms around her legs, lifting her entire body out of the water. I toss her over my shoulder, so she splashes back down.

When she pops up, through her laughter, she says, "You're a violent mermaid."

"Think of me more like a shark."

"Guess I better try to outrun you then, huh?"

"You can try," I taunt.

I have no idea how long I spend chasing after her, swimming back and forth, listening to her laugh every time she'd come up for air. I don't know if we're annoying people around us, and quite frankly, I don't give a fuck if we are. We're having too much fun to stop.

Underneath the water, I lose Shay. I look around, trying to figure out where she went. I take a moment to come up for air, and while I shake the water from my eyes, I feel a hand grip my cock through my trunks.

I glance around, trying to make sure no one's paying attention. Thankfully, everybody is in their own worlds.

When Shay pops up from the water, I say, "You're apparently a dirty mermaid."

She shrugs. "Just trying to release the kraken."

Pulling her close, I say, "Later on, I'm going to fuck the shit out of you."

She sighs. "Promises, promises."

And off she swims once again.

A little while later, Dan and Becky join us in the water. Becky prances around on her tiptoes, attempting to get used to the cool temperature. Finally, Dan has had enough and dunks his fiancé.

I expect her to be pissed, but she just laughs it off. It's good to see them having fun and not taking the wedding too seriously. I remember when Dan and Becky got together, they were always laughing. I hope when the wedding's over, they get back to that.

Dan drops under the water, swimming between Becky's legs and popping up with her sitting on his shoulders.

"Come on, Dev. Let's play some Chicken."

"Oh, no," I begin. "I don't think Shay—"

Shay interrupts. "Sure, let's do it."

Man, she's up for anything.

Can't wait to put that to the test more tonight.

"Come on, Cassanova," Shay prompts. "Lift me up."

"Yes, ma'am," I reply before doing as she asks.

When she's comfortably on my shoulders, she says, "I'm so tall. Ha, watch this!" She bends over a little so that her tits are resting on the top of my head.

I start laughing so hard I struggle to keep my balance.

Shay grabs my ears as though trying to steer me. "Focus, Devon! It's game time."

When I finally stop laughing, Dan and I take our positions, ready to let the girls attempt to knock each other off.

One of the bridesmaids yells, "Ready? Set? Go!"

Dan and I attempt to hold on to the women as they lock fingertips, trying to knock each other down. We can't see much—mainly just each other. I worry things may be getting a little heated between Shay and Becky, but my fears are quieted when I hear them laughing.

It isn't much longer before I see Becky come toppling down into the water, making a big splash around her. Shay celebrates while still on my shoulders.

Dan's sister, Wendy, and her boyfriend decide that they want to go next. The fight's even shorter, and Shay still comes out on top.

No surprise there.

What *is* surprising is who wants to go next. Kyra and her boyfriend, Chad.

No fucking way.

I'm about to draw a harsh line in the sand, but Shay yanks on my ears again, telling me to stop talking.

Kyra gets on Chad's shoulders, muttering, "This should be easy."

I hear Shay retort, "Bring it on, Barbie."

"Let's go, Morticia."

Without any further warning, they begin. If I thought it was hard to hold onto Shay with Becky, this is worse. It's like trying to stay on a bucking bronco...expect opposite, I guess. Shay must be struggling too because her thighs press against the sides of my head, attempting to trap me in a death grip.

I'm still not able to see what's going on, but I take cues from the crowd of people now gathered around and shouting.

One of them yells, "Whoa, Kyra! No nails!"

What the fuck is going on up there?

Everyone starts cheering way louder, and I hear what sounds like a slap. I'm about to put a stop to this before someone gets hurt, but in that same moment, I see Kyra come crashing down.

Wanting to look Shay over, I sink under the water, putting her back on her feet.

When I come back to the surface, I ask, "Are you okay?"

She's retying the strings on her swimsuit. "I'm good. The bitch tried to pull my top off."

It's then that I see the nail marks on Shay's forearms. Snapping my head around to Kyra, I bite, "What the fuck is wrong with you?"

With an evil smile, she says, "We were just having some fun. I would've won if she wasn't built like a damn tank."

"Oh, come on, Kyra!"

Shay puts her hand on my chest to stop me. "Babe, it's fine. Let her throw her fits. It's all she has."

I'm ready to dig my heels in and keep giving Kyra some hell, but hearing Shay call me babe catches me off-guard. I know this whole thing's just an act, but it's still nice.

She holds out her hand for mine. When I take it, I grab my hat, putting it back on my head before she leads me to the hot tub. We're the only two in, so we take a seat on a bench along one edge.

"Are you sure you're okay?" I ask, grabbing Shay's arms and looking them over.

"I'm fine. I promise." She pulls her arms back. "Quit fussing over me."

"What if I want to fuss over you?"

"Don't. I'm a big girl. I can fend for myself."

"I know you can. Doesn't mean there's anything wrong with someone else looking out for you too."

She just looks away, not responding to my comment.

And before I can go any further, I feel her fingers lightly rubbing against my cock through my swim trunks.

"Shay," I warn. "What do you think you're doing?"

"Oh, just playing."

I exhale a sharp breath as she gives it a squeeze. Leaning my head back on the side of the hot tub, I try to focus enough to keep my composure.

But fuck, it's hard.

No pun intended.

"What's wrong?" She asks, trying to act innocent.

Before I can answer, a group of people come to join us. I figure Shay will stop her teasing, but with the jets causing bubbles across the surface, anything she's doing is completely hidden.

Because of that, she seems to have no plans to stop. Her fingers still tease my cock, which is now aching to break free. She alternates between stroking me and then teasing just the head.

My mind struggles to think of something else. *Anything* else.

Think of baseball. Has the word ball in it. Shay's tickling my balls.

Think of dogs. Nothing sexual there. Except doggy-style. I want to fuck Shay doggy-style.

Fuck. There's no use.

I'm screwed.

No, you wish you were getting screwed right now.

When even more people get in to join us, things are getting a bit more crowded.

Shay decides to scoot into my lap to make sure there's room for everyone. When she's comfortable, she wiggles around a little bit, rubbing her ass against me.

Seeing an opportunity to get some payback, I use my knee to hold her legs open while my fingers tease her clit through her bathing suit. I can feel her holding her breath as I continue to play.

As crazy as I may be driving her, when she wiggles her ass again, I realize she still has the advantage.

Thankfully, we aren't the only couple that seem to be all over each other. Dan's sister and her boyfriend are whispering sweet nothings in each other's ears, and even Dan and Becky are practically making out.

Meanwhile, Kyra and Chad still sit by themselves at the big table where we all ate.

Thank God.

When Shay grinds against me, I say, "I can't wait to fuck you later."

She gives a sly grin but doesn't say anything.

Dan's sister, Wendy, gets everyone's attention and says, "Let's play Truth or Dare."

Everyone looks a little hesitant except Dan who says, "Okay, I'll go first."

"Devon, truth or dare?"

Why me?

"Uhh, truth," I reply, not wanting to have to do anything that would potentially require me to stand up right now.

Dan thinks for a moment before asking, "What's the thing you like most about Shay?"

"Do you mean physical or like personality?"

"Both."

I think, trying to come up with an answer that could potentially get Becky off our backs.

"Personality wise, I'd say it's how unapologetic she is about always being *exactly* who she is." I say the words, seemingly putting on a good show. But the truth is I mean every word. To lighten things back up, I add, "As for the physical, her boobs. Hands down."

That gets a laugh from everyone, including Shay. And then, she gives my cock a firm squeeze, causing me to grit my teeth, barely able to contain myself.

Next, someone else takes a turn. When Becky picks dare, the guy taunts her to make out with one of her friends from college.

Much to my surprise, Becky does it without argument. Dan's eyes get so big that he looks like a kid at Christmas.

I bet that will be some prime material for his spank bank. It's not doing much for me, but I'm glad Dan gets some enjoyment out of it.

A few other people go, mainly picking truth. I don't pay much attention to what any of them are saying because Shay is still teasing.

I'm ready to get the fuck out of here and bury my cock so deep into Shay that she can barely walk tomorrow. But it might look weird if we just bounce out of nowhere.

I'm pulled out of my fantasies when Wendy decides she's going to pose the question to Shay. "Truth or dare?"

Without hesitation, she answers, "Dare."

Why is that not surprising?

Wendy taps her finger on her chin, trying to come up with something good. When she gets a wicked smile on her face, I fear what she settled on.

"I dare you to take that cute boyfriend of yours over to one of those empty chairs and give him your best lap dance."

Really? Of course, that's the stripper's dare. And what's with everyone being so horny? A couple more drinks and rounds of this game, and we're all likely to end up in an orgy.

"Come on," I say. "Really?"

Shay stands up and holds out her hand for mine. I tell her, "We don't have to."

She shrugs. "I know."

I take her hand and thank my lucky stars that my cock has gone down before I rise from the water. Something tells me it's about to spring back to life, though.

She pulls a chair away from the others and tells me to sit.

I do, and the DJ, who's been playing popular hits in the background all night, plays Pour Some Sugar on Me.

Oh, this just keeps getting better.

I expect Shay to play the whole thing off as a joke, so I'm shocked when she starts swaying her hips and walking toward me. When she reaches me, she stops, turns, and bends over, giving me a perfect view of her ass before sitting in my lap and starting to grind. She gyrates with the beat of the music.

Mind you, I've had lap dances before. In fact, before Kyra, I went to strip clubs quite a bit. It was a decent way to spend a Friday night, but lap dances were always a little meh. The whole *look but don't touch* idea sort of put a damper on things.

Shay grinding on my cock, though, is so much better.

Because there's one paramount difference.

With Shay, I don't have to keep my hands to myself.

Gently pushing her forward, I stand up and grab her by the hand.

I announce to everyone, "Sorry, folks. Peep show's over. We're continuing this in our room.

They all groan but quickly get back to Truth or Dare.

Shay says, "'I'm not done."

Picking her up and tossing her over my shoulder, I say, "The fuck you aren't."

Chapter Fourteen

SHAY

T easing Devon all day really paid off. The animalistic look in his eyes shows he wants to fuck me like crazy. I wanted to turn him feral to see how dirty he would get. Now, I prepare to hang on for the wild ride.

"I can walk," I tell Devon as he still carries me like a sack of potatoes over his shoulder.

"Not fast enough," he practically growls.

"Why the big hurry?"

"Shay with the way you were teasing me, you're lucky I don't fuck you right here in the middle of the hallway."

"Ohhhh, sounds fun."

He lets out a heavy sigh, and I know I'm still driving him crazy.

When we get to the room, he flies through the door and sets me on my feet when we are inside. I barely have time to process anything before

Devon's mouth crashes down on mine. He kisses me so hard and fast that I barely even realize that his hands are pulling my bathing suit from my body.

When I'm naked, he commands, "Get your sexy ass on the bed."

Not quite done teasing, I get on all fours with my ass up in the air, shaking it like I'm waving a red cape in front of a bull.

Next thing I feel is his hand come down to give a firm smack to my ass. I want him to do it again, but he leaves me and disappears into the bathroom.

What the hell is he up to?

When he comes back, I see that he has the tie from one of the fuzzy bathrobes in his hand.

In a stern voice, he says, "Get on your back, and put your hands above your head."

I'm all for a little bondage especially because I know how great the sex is with Devon. Being tied up while he does dirty things to my naked body is enough to give me tingly feelings all over.

He spends the next couple of minutes, tying my hands together and making sure it's tight enough to hold me in place. He hooks the knot over the headboard before stepping back to admire his work.

His eyes rake over me like he can't decide exactly where he wants to start. He still wears only his swim trunks, which his cock is doing its best to burst out of.

The bed sinks as he gets on his knees and starts to move toward me. Stopping in front of my legs, he pushes my knees open and gazes down at the sweet spot between them.

Taking his finger and lightly running it down my slit, he says, "Do you think it's nice to tease me all night?"

"It was fun," I say with a grin.

"Are you ready for some payback?"

"Abso-fucking-lutely."

He takes the pad of his middle finger and applies some pressure to my clit as he rubs small circles. The touch is just enough to make me squirm against the fuzzy restraint.

"How much do you think you can take?" Devon asks.

"However much you can dish out," I taunt, hoping he's going to give me everything he's got.

He yanks his fingers away before moving down so his mouth is even with my pussy. Leaning forward, he gives my clit a soft kiss, making me release a long moan.

Before he gets going, he flips the baseball cap on his head backwards.

Oh my gosh, the rumors were true.

It's like seeing an animal in its natural habitat. Beautiful yet fucking wild.

Now that he has better access, his mouth starts eating me out. He sucks and licks in such a way that I feel like my brain has turned to mush. And the lower half of my body can't seem to sit still. Devon takes care of that, though, linking his arms around my thighs to keep me in place—and to hold me open for him.

My hands tug on the rope, desperate to be able to grab onto anything and everything. But he expertly tied this. Like a fucking Boy Scout.

Just another thing Devon Samson excels at.

I wonder if he would get a merit badge for his excellent tongue skills.

Pulling me even closer to him, he buries his face between my lower lips. His tongue teases my entrance before moving up to flick against my piercing and then back again. After teasing, he gives all his attention to my clit, sucking on and licking it at the same time.

My thighs start to quiver in his hands, and I feel the orgasm about to take hold. I prepare myself to hold on for the ride, but before I can fly over the edge, he stops.

"What are you doing?" I moan.

"Don't you recognize some teasing when you see it?" He looks up at me with a wicked grin and fiery eyes.

"Oh, that's not fair."

"Neither is giving me blue balls all day," he says with a light smack to my clit.

The action makes my legs buck off the bed, but quickly, Devon holds them down once more and goes back to eating me out. He does the same thing as before, slowly building me up and bringing me right to the edge before stopping.

Every nerve in my body has roared to life. At this point, Devon could probably just blow on me, and I'd lose it.

"Do you think I should let you come?" He asks, planting a light kiss on my clit between each word.

"Yes, please." I draw out the second word.

"Do you think you deserve it?"

"I'll do anything," I beg.

I've never felt more ready to explode in my life. My clit throbs, blood pumping to it and making it even more sensitive.

"Are you going to stop teasing me?" He asks.

I answer honestly. "Probably not."

I can tell he's smiling. "Good girl."

With that, he goes back to licking. But this time, he doesn't stop. This time, he keeps going until my entire body quakes with my orgasm. My pussy pulses while Devon continues to lick. I try my hardest to get my hands free, but it's still no use.

I moan so loudly that I'm sure whoever our neighbors are can hear us.

But I don't give a fuck. This feels too damn good to keep quiet.

After coming for what feels like forever, I say, "That was amazing."

"We aren't done yet."

Before I can ask what he has in mind, he sits up on his knees and angles himself to the side of me. I figure he's getting ready to fuck me, but he has other plans. He takes his two middle fingers and slides them inside me, curving them upward. He starts stroking that sweet spot inside. A lot of guys couldn't find the g-spot with GPS, but Devon seems to be able to zero in on it like he's got radar or something.

"Oh, fuck," I moan as I realize how good it feels.

He begins slowly, but soon enough, his fingers are moving harder and faster. The only sounds that fill the air around us are my moans and the wet sounds my pussy makes. Pressure starts to build inside my core, and I'm anxious to release it.

"Are you ready to come again, Sunshine?"

"God, yes."

His lips pull into a half-smile. "You can call me Devon."

Before I can tell him how lame his joke is, he uses his other hand to rub my clit. There is no slow build up. He moves in frenzied motions, and it's enough to make the pressure inside me boil over. Devon continues to rub me but pulls his fingers out, causing my pussy to gush all over the bed.

I've gotten off plenty of times with guys fingering me. I'm no stranger to g-spot orgasms, but the squirting is new.

I like it.

And apparently, Devon does too.

His eyes watch my pussy the entire time before he mumbles, "That is so fucking hot."

"Fuck me," I plead.

I think he's going to keep teasing, but he surprises me by leaning up and untying my wrists. Once my hands are free, he immediately stands up to take his trunks off.

"Get on your hands and knees," he says. "Show me that sexy ass."

I do as he wishes and position myself head down and ass up. I can't see what he's doing, but I hear the familiar sound of him opening the condom. Moments later, I feel him sliding into me from behind.

I love doggy style.

Maybe it's that I feel like there's less emotional connection involved in it.

Or maybe that it just feels incredible.

Either way, it's my favorite.

Devon grips onto my hips while he begins slamming into me. He told me he wanted to fuck the shit out of me, and he wasn't lying.

I arch my back in an attempt to pull him even deeper into me, prompting Devon to reach forward and grab my hair. He gently pulls while he continues to move at a quick pace.

"Come here," he says, pulling me so that I'm sitting up on my knees with my back pressed against his chest.

He slows his pace a little, forcing us both to savor this moment. One hand holds me by the throat, holding me still so he can kiss and bite the back of my neck. His other moves between my legs to play with my clit, which is still hypersensitive.

When he holds it between his two fingers and moves up and down. Devon whispers in my ear, "Come on, beautiful. I know you have one more for me. Come on this cock again."

Between his dick, his fingers, and his dirty mouth, it doesn't take me long before I'm obeying his command and riding the waves of pleasure once again.

Devon's arms wrap around me tight as he struggles to stay upright as he fills the condom. "Fuuuuuck," he groans before we both collapse in a heap on the bed.

Looking over at me, he says, "Sorry if I was too rough."

"Are you kidding? I loved it. I'm going to have to tease you more often."

He stands up to go throw the condom away, and I get started positioning the extra pillows that will go between us. Three orgasms or not, we still aren't going to cuddle.

When he comes back, I ask, "So, what's on the gameplan tomorrow? Please tell me it's something relaxing."

"Well, yours is. The girls are doing a brunch and spa day while the guys go and play some basketball."

"You play basketball?" I ask.

"Sure. I mean, not well, but I try."

He goes on to say something else, but I'm so tired that I don't hear a single word of it. Before he even finishes his sentence, I'm fast asleep.

Chapter Fifteen

DEVON

After passing out and sleeping like the dead last night, I'm awoken my something warm and wet wrapped around my cock.

By far, my *favorite* way in the world to be woken up.

My eyes shoot open, and I look down to see Shay between my legs, on her knees with her ass in the air. Her blue eyes look up at me while she takes the head of my dick and slaps it against her tongue—which I just realize has her tongue ring in it. She must have just put it back in.

And holy fuck, she knows just how to use it.

Grabbing a pillow, I prop it behind my head to get a better view of what she's doing. I don't want to miss a single second of my cock sliding in and out of her mouth.

Still looking at me with wide eyes, Shay circles the head, dragging the metal ball of her tongue ring along the sensitive flesh. Motherfucker, she's so sexy.

A piece of hair falls into her face, and I reach down to push it out of the way. When it happens again, she seems to have had enough of her unruly hair and quickly sits up to throw it up in a bun on top of her head.

Then, she gets back to work. This time, she seems even more intense than before.

"Fuck, Shay," I groan as my eyes stay fixed on the way she's now lightly sucking on the head while her tongue still teases.

One of her hands reaches down to lightly run her fingernails along my balls. The soft touches make goosebumps pop up all over my skin.

Shay with her ass in the air and my cock in her mouth is maybe my favorite thing I've ever seen. It's top three for sure.

She keeps teasing, driving me crazy with every lick of her tongue until finally a switch flips inside her, and she starts sucking my cock like some kind of damn porn star.

Good God, the woman basically unhinges her jaw in order to take me down her throat. She fits the whole fucking thing in her mouth. I'm seriously impressed. I may not have the longest dick, but it's pretty thick. Most of the blowjobs I get are just women focusing on the head—which is fine. Any time a woman offers to touch my penis, I don't complain about how she does it.

But Shay?

Shay is a breed all her own.

She takes me down her throat while using her tongue ring to tease the sensitive spot underneath. One of her hands continues to play with my balls, and the other strokes me.

As much as I'd love to stay here and watch her all day, with the way she's blowing me, there's no way I'm going to last much longer.

"Sunshine," I moan. "Do you want me to fuck you?" I love some head, but I know she'd probably rather I fuck her. That way, we both get something out of it.

She pulls my head out of her mouth for a moment, and I think she's going to take me up on my offer, but she just replies with, "No, this time, it's all about you."

Have I mentioned Shay just might be the perfect woman?

She goes back to sucking with a clear goal in mind: to make me come so hard I lose my fucking mind.

Her hand squeezes a little harder as she increases her tempo. I feel my balls starting to tighten, and I tell her I'm about to come. I always like to announce it.

No one enjoys that type of surprise, and I don't want her to take it in her mouth if she doesn't want to.

But she keeps going.

Sucking harder and faster.

Before I know it, she holds my cock in her mouth while I shoot my load directly down her throat.

She sits up as her thumb wipes off her bottom lip.

"Holy shit, Shay," I say, out of breath like I've just run a damn marathon. "I don't know what I did to deserve that but thank you."

"Well, I figure you are way ahead of me in the *orgasms given* column, so maybe I owed you one."

Okay, we are going to put an end to that thinking right now.

Grabbing her, I pull her down next to me and get on top of her so that my face is down by hers. "Now, you listen here, little lady. This is not a competition. It's not a *who can one up the other?* I *love* eating your pussy and giving you orgasms. And every single time I do it, I never expect anything in return. Ever. I don't care if I make you come a hundred times this week, you don't owe me shit. You hear me?"

She nods. "I still want you to feel good, too."

"And I appreciate that. I fucking love it. But don't think that you need to keep up with me because I promise you that by the end of the week, your orgasm count will be much higher than mine."

I wouldn't have it any other way.

"Oh, come on, man! That was a total foul!" I yell at Dan as he pushes into me as he makes his way to shoot the basketball.

He still misses the shot and says "You can't call fouls on me. I'm the groom."

115

"You know, I think you are really milking this whole groom thing. I've heard of the bride getting whatever she wants but not you."

He points his finger at me. "Hey, Becky has gotten her way on absolutely everything. You will let me have a few fouls."

Everyone else who was playing with us is already sitting on the bench, so Dan and I start just tossing the ball back and forth and taking random shots.

As we are walking, I say, "So, are you nervous about the big day?"

He shakes his head. "Nah. I knew pretty early on that Becky was the one I wanted to marry. I'm ready to finally make it official."

"How'd you know?" I ask. "I mean, that she was the one."

"Life with her was so much better than without her, and I never wanted to go back to the without her part."

Makes sense, I guess.

He asks, "Is it weird being here with Kyra?"

"Weird? Kind of. Annoying? Definitely. She's been absolutely awful to Shay."

His eyes go wide. "Yeah, dude, I saw them playing chicken yesterday. What was up with Kyra? She went total apeshit."

"Fuck, I don't know. But if she's not careful, Shay's going to kick her ass before the week is done."

He thinks for a moment. "I think I'd like to see that."

"You and me both—although I don't know how much of Kyra would be left when it was all said and done."

"I'm honestly kind of surprised that Kyra and Shay haven't had any contact before now."

I'm about to ask why, but I quickly remember that Shay and I are supposed to be actually dating—not just pretending and casually fucking for a week.

"Kyra and I haven't talked much at all since we broke up. She made it very clear she wanted me to leave her the fuck alone, so that's what I did."

"Do you ever miss her?" He asks. "Or I guess I should ask did you miss her before you got with Shay?"

"No."

"Really?" He seems surprised. "Why?"

"Because unlike you and Becky, I quickly realized my life was better *without* Kyra. It just took me getting away from her to realize it."

Stepping closer to me, Dan asks, "So, are you and Shay the real thing? Come on, you can tell me if this is just some sort of elaborate plan."

Dan and I don't usually have secrets, but I hate to say that this is going to be one of them. I'm not about to put him in a position where he has to choose if he's going to lie to his new bride. One of us lying is better than two. Plus, I'm not sure if he actually would lie for me. Dan is awful at keeping secrets, and he may go and blab to her.

I'm not about to take that chance, so I say, "No, it's the real deal. Shay's awesome, and I'm crazy about her."

He smiles. "Almost like you can't imagine your life without her?"

I try to just shrug off his words because in regard to my situation, they're ridiculous. Shay has made it abundantly clear that she's not looking for anything beyond this week. Hell, she won't even cuddle with me. So, I imagine that when this wedding is over, we will go back to what we were before.

Friends?

Acquaintances?

Bartender and customer?

I'm not sure what to call it, but I know that my life will go back to being primarily *without* her.

I do my best to ignore the pang of sadness that I feel at that thought. Shay and I have only been here a couple of days, but already, she's completely altered the way I think of her. Underneath her tough cold exterior, there's someone who is weird in the best way possible. She keeps me laughing and even more so keeps me on my toes.

Maybe leaving her at the end of this week will be harder than I thought.

Chapter Sixteen

SHAY

*W*hat the hell is the point of these cucumbers over my eyes. They keep sliding off, and I'm positive they aren't doing a damn thing for my skin.

I've never been much of a spa gal. Sure, I get the appeal of it, but it's weird to me to sit in a pristine room with a bunch of other women and get pampered. I'd rather be sitting in my living room, doing an at-home facial while my dog and I watch crappy TV.

But here I am.

And right now, I have no Devon here to be a buffer.

I don't know any of these women really, and even if I did, I doubt this is how I would choose to spend time with them. Overall, I don't have a lot of female friends anyway. I tend to get along better with the male persuasion. Less drama.

If Devon and I were really dating, though, I would be making an effort to get to know these people. I'd be trying really hard to fit in and get them to like me. Maybe I should be making that same effort now to try to get them to believe the story that we're selling.

Okay, I'll try. But I can't do it with the fucking cucumbers.

Taking them off my eyes, I look around and see that most of the other women have done the same. Well, that would have been nice to know earlier.

Just when I'm about to insert myself into the conversation and try to be more social, someone comes out to tell me that it's my turn for a massage.

Guess the conversation will have to wait.

I follow the women into a room that's dimly lit by a small lamp and a bunch of candles.

In a soothing voice, she asks, "What kind of music would you like to listen to?"

My smartass mouth answers before my brain has time to process what I'm saying. "Cotton-eyed Joe."

She gives a confused, "What?"

This time, I reply with, "You choose. I'm fine with anything."

Five minutes later, I'm lying on her table, half comatose in a state of relaxation. I had to wear my swimsuit since I forgot all my underwear, and I didn't want to get a massage completely naked. I try to get my mind to focus and think of what I could talk to the girls about when I get back.

But the massage feels so good that I can't focus on anything except how heavy my eyelids are getting. I think towards the end, I actually do nod off for a bit.

When I'm relaxed enough to be compared to a limp noodle, I head back to join everyone else. No cucumbers remain, and everyone is now drinking bloody Mary's around one of the tables. There isn't an extra seat for me, so I head over to sit in one of the lounge chairs.

So much for me trying to be social.

I lean back and play with the tie of the bathrobe. Instantly, I'm transported back to last night when Devon had me tied up with this thing. Good lord, the man knows *exactly* what he's doing in the bedroom. He had me a little surprised when he tied me up. I didn't know any type of *kinky* would be in Devon's wheelhouse, but I'm glad it was. I wonder exactly how much other stuff he has done.

Threesome?

Anal?

Maybe I should ask him.

Or maybe I don't want to know the answer.

I've had a decent amount of sex in my life—most of it nothing to write home about. So, when a guy suggests trying something new, I typically go for it because you never know what might feel good. With Devon, though, I think that even the vanilla is something to write home about.

He is living proof that practice makes perfect.

My mind begins to wander, thinking about what he may have in store for me tonight. I'm hoping this spa doesn't go too long because I'd much rather skip ahead to the dirty stuff.

Just when I'm getting lost in my own world, Becky walks over to me, handing me a bloody Mary. "Here." She smiles. "Figured you might need this. I know how hard it is trying to hang out with a bunch of people you don't know."

"Bless you," I say with a small laugh as I take the drink.

To my surprise, she sits down on the chair next to me.

Here we go.

Stirring her own drink with the celery stalk that hangs out of it, she begins to speak. "Man, you've really gotten under Kyra's skin, huh?"

I give an awkward laugh. "Yeah, she's no fan of mine."

"I know she seems...well, she seems like a bitch. And I guess sometimes, she can be, but underneath all that, there really is a good person."

I look over at her. "I don't think she's a terrible person. I'm sure she's a great friend to you. I'm her ex's new girlfriend, so it makes sense that she hates me. I can take whatever she wants to dish out. What gets me going is when she's mean to Devon. From what I hear, *she* is the one who dumped *him.*"

Becky nods. "You're right. I'm not really sure why she's so awful to him. She broke up with Devon and told him to leave her alone. If I'm being honest, I think it kind of pissed her off that he actually listened."

"You think she wanted him to pine for her?"

"I don't know. Something like that, I guess. Maybe she wanted him to fight for her." She looks at me again and adds, "I don't blame him, though. He fought for that relationship for three years."

"Do you think there's any feelings left between them?" I'm not sure exactly why I ask the question. Yes, it helps our fake relationship look more real, but I'm also curious.

Why do I care?

After this week, I don't give a shit if they get back together or not. For all I care, they can get married and have little Devon and Kyra babies.

Even as I think the words, I know I'm full of shit. It would piss me off if he got back with her—not because I want him, of course, but because Kyra doesn't deserve a guy like Devon.

"No, I think those two are about as done as two people can get."

Becky finishes downing the liquid in the bottom of her glass. Before she can even set it on the table, someone has appeared with a fresh one to hand to her.

She switches out the glasses and says, "I swear being a bride is amazing. Next week, I'm not going to know what to do with myself when there's no one there to wait on me hand and foot."

Joking, I reply, "That's what Dan is for."

She giggles. "That's a good point." She takes another drink. "Maybe it's that I'm on my third one of these, but I'm going to be honest with you about something."

Great.

123

She goes on. "I'm still not sure if you and Devon are the real thing. Part of me still thinks the two of you are bullshitting, but I can't deny that you two seem to have serious chemistry."

I have no idea how to respond to that. I feel like she's trying to trap me into saying the wrong thing. I opt for, "We're crazy about each other."

"I *know* that this question is the alcohol talking, but I just have to know. Is his nickname around town accurate?"

I can't help but smile. "Oh, Becky, it's so true that he should legally change it to that."

"Damn," she whispers before turning to me. "Don't get the wrong idea here. Devon's not my type, but when you hear multiple women talking about how good his *skills* are, it gets a girl wondering."

She stands up and holds out her hand for mine. "Come on, let's go sit with the other girls."

"There's no more seats," I argue.

"Watch this." She then calls, "We need another chair at the main table."

Immediately, one of the workers accommodates her wishes, and another chair is squeezed in.

She smiles. "See? Perks of being a bride."

As we get to the table, she says, "Make room, everyone. Shay is going to join us."

Kyra rolls her eyes and scoffs. But as though the lord is looking out for me, someone comes out and calls her back for her massage. She looks almost hesitant to go as though she's going to miss something while she's gone, but she still walks off with the masseuse.

Shelly looks at me, and says, "I still can't figure out where I know you from."

We're back to this?

"Well, Shelly, you have a few more days to figure it out," I say with a wink.

Dan's sister, Wendy, says, "Okay, Shay, spill the details."

"About?"

"We watched your man carry you off like a damn caveman last night. Did he follow through when you got back to the room?"

I'm not usually one to kiss and tell. The only person who gets any type of details is Suzie, and even then, she has to drag them out of me. But right now, every single woman around the table is staring at me, waiting for my story.

"Oh yeah," I say. "It was amazing."

The way they are sitting silently, still staring lets me know that what I just said isn't going to satisfy them.

I clear my throat, trying to buy myself a little bit of time. I try to think of something to say without giving away too many details. As great as the sex is with Devon, it's something that's between us, and I'd like to keep it that way. It's like a dirty little secret that only he and I know.

But I have to give them something.

I settle on, "Let's just say that I bet his tongue is tired today—if you get my meaning."

They all let out a collective, jealous groan.

Yeah, eat your hearts out, ladies. Devon will be eating out me.

Thankfully, someone changes the subject, and most of them start talking amongst themselves. I exhale a heavy sigh, thankful that the attention is no longer on me.

But of course, I'm not going to get off that easy.

Wendy leans in close to me, "I've known Devon a long time. He and Dan have been friends their whole lives. I know sometimes he gets the reputation of a man whore, but he's really a good guy."

"Yeah, he is," I agree.

"And for what it's worth, I can see how much he likes you. I've never seen him look at anyone the way he looks at you—even Kyra, and they were together for three years."

"Really?" I ask, genuinely curious.

"Really. I can tell how much he loves you."

That word...*love*...makes my stomach churn. I've only said that world romantically to one man in my life, and it turned out that he definitely wasn't worth it. Now, even the mention of it gets me to high tail it in the other direction. As much as Devon is the exact opposite of my ex, I don't want to associate him with the L word either.

I try to calm myself down, though, because clearly, Devon doesn't love me. There's no way in hell.

He's just a really, really good actor.

Hm. Maybe he and my ex have something in common after all.

"Hey, you," Devon greets with a big smile as I make my way to the table on the patio. All of the guys are back from basketball, showered and waiting for us.

Thankfully, the rest of the spa day went off without incident. Kyra and I didn't have to share much time together since we were always called for different treatments at different times. I'm sure that was Becky's plan to try to avoid the drama. And I did a pretty decent job at being social with everyone else. Aside from Kyra, all of the other women were surprisingly lovely.

"Hey," I say, leaning down to give him a quick peck on the lips.

Is it weird that I actually missed him?

"You okay?" He asks.

"I'm good. Everything was fine."

"How was the spa? Did you get all rubbed and scrubbed?"

I laugh. "Something like that."

Leaning forward, he asks, "Can I rub you later?"

Unable to control my smile, I answer, "Depends on where you want to rub."

Moving even closer, he says, "Everywhere."

I feel the heat shoot directly to my pussy. I changed into a sundress before coming down, and I lost the swimsuit. So, under this dress, I'm wearing no underwear yet again.

I know Devon must be aware of that fact by the way his hand starts traveling up my thigh, getting a little closer to my pussy with every pass.

"You're not playing fair," I whisper.

"I know."

Dinner is just one course this time—steak, baked potatoes, and green beans. It's not nearly as fancy as the dinner on our first night here. I'm grateful for that since after an entire day around other people, I'm anxious to get some alone time with just Devon and myself.

Sure, the sex sounds great, but it's not just that.

I'm ready to be around someone I don't have to pretend in front of. I can be myself without wondering how everyone else perceives me.

Not to mention the fact that it's hard to concentrate on anything besides how close Devon's hand is now to my pussy. Thank goodness no one can see what's going on under this tablecloth.

We dig in, trying to get finished as fast as we can without making it too obvious.

When we are just about done, Wendy says, "Devon, we got to know your lovely girlfriend today. You better not let this one go."

Devon moves his hand from my thigh and puts it around my shoulders. "Oh, I don't plan on it."

Becky now chimes in. "Yeah, Devon. We all like her. If you two decide to break up, we are keeping her and getting rid of you."

He leans close enough to whisper, "I think you may have actually convinced Becky. I'm impressed."

"Don't count your chickens just yet." When he looks at me, I add, "I'll tell you later."

A couple other women jump in, telling Devon how awesome they think I am. I'm loving them stroking my ego, but Kyra is waiting in the wings to bring me back down to Earth.

"You're all kidding, right?" She says with a disgusted look on her face. "You can't all really believe that Devon would be with a girl like her."

Before I can ask it, Wendy does. "A girl like what?

Kyra gestures at me. "Well, look at her. She looks like she's just escaped from prison with all her tattoos and dark makeup. She probably has a criminal record a mile long. I don't know if Devon is desperate or if he's just in some sort of depression since I dumped him, but the guy I dated wouldn't give a girl like Shay even more than a second look."

Devon interrupts her, "Kyra, I'm not the guy you dated. Not even close. I don't let anyone walk all over me anymore the way you used to. You want to know why I started dating Shay? Because she treats me like an actual person instead of a piece of garbage. I don't have to try to convince her why she should be with me."

His words make me realize just how much Kyra hurt him when they broke up—and when they were together for that matter. I'm fairly sure that in the past few days, I've been better to Devon than Kyra was when they were together. That may be a big leap to make but judging by the hurt look on Devon's face right now, maybe not.

He goes on to add, "Shay is the coolest girl I've ever met, and she's ten times the woman you'll ever be."

Kyra gets a smug smile on her face. "Look, if you want to date the fat loser, that's up to you."

"Hey! Enough!" Devon shouts.

I'm perfectly capable of standing up for myself, and quite frankly, I don't give a shit what Kyra has to say. She's just miserable. But it's nice hearing Devon stick up for me. I don't have many people in my life who would do that for me.

He stands up while grabbing my hand, wanting me to follow him. As we leave the table, he turns toward Becky, "Get your friend in check. I'm serious, Beck. Enough is enough."

Without waiting for her response, we head away from the patio.

Looking up at him, I ask, "What do you want to do?"

As we pass by the bar, he grabs a bottle of tequila when the bartender has his back turned.

"I have an idea."

Chapter Seventeen

DEVON

"I'm really sorry about Kyra," I say to Shay, who sits across from me in the oversized bathtub, covered in bubbles and half-drunk on tequila.

"Devon, stop apologizing. It's not your fault at all."

"I know, but no one should talk to you like that."

The side of her mouth pulls up into a smile. "Babe, once again, I grew up as a goth girl in a small town with two gay dads. I'm no stranger to people slinging insults at me."

Biting my fingernail, I say, "It still doesn't make it right."

Her face falls a little. "No, it doesn't, but it is what it is. I learned a long time ago to just let things roll off my shoulders. Most people are assholes to others because they're unhappy with something in their own lives. Kyra is no different. I'm pretty sure she has a lot to be unhappy with."

"What do you mean?"

She takes another sip of tequila straight out of the bottle before handing it to me. I swear the woman is going to drink me under the table.

Shay doesn't even make a face when taking a drink of the strong, clear liquid. I, on the other hand, look like a baby trying something sour for the first time.

She starts talking again, "Well, clearly, Kyra isn't happy with that new man of hers. She dumped a really great guy for a total douchebag, and she's just now realizing what a mistake she made. She thinks that someone like me ended up with the one she let get away, and that eats at her."

I stop her, "Wait a minute...did you just call me a great guy?"

She may roll her eyes, but I still get a laugh out of her. "Eh, you're alright, I guess."

I have no plans of letting her forget what she said, but I pivot a little and ask, "Why do you think Kyra is so unhappy with her new guy?"

Now, Shay's eyes avoid mine. "Let's just say that I recognize that look she gets when dealing with him. I've been there before."

That small little tidbit right there is the most that Shay has given me about her past. The tequila must be loosening her up a little.

Deciding to try to get more out of her, I shoot my shot. "Shay, tell me about your ex."

"What ex?" She asks, trying to dance around the question.

"The one who makes you have some sort of weird connection to Kyra. The one who fucked you up so bad you won't even cuddle after sex now."

She goes quiet for an abnormally long time. I think she is just ignoring me and hoping the question goes away. I'm about to say something else when she surprises me by finally starting to speak.

"His name is Alan. I was a senior in college when I met him. He was one of my professors. He was about thirty-five at the time."

Already, I'm not liking where this story is heading.

"He saw me listening to music one day, asked what it was, and said he loved that same band. He wanted to know if I wanted to go get coffee and talk about it. A few hours later, we were back in his place in bed together."

She stops to take a breath. "We started dating, and I was head-over-heels for him. He seemed so much deeper than any of the other high school or college guys I had dated. He made me all these promises. We were going to move in together, travel the world, and then, get married and have kids. On the outside, everything was perfect, but something just felt a little off. Every time I'd ask him about it, he'd just tell me I was young and too insecure. I didn't want to lose him, so I'd just sweep it under the rug."

"One day, he comes to me and says that we need to talk. He confessed that there was someone else. He said he'd been seeing her the whole time he was seeing me, and he loved both of us. He didn't know which he wanted to choose, but he was coming clean to both of us, and he hoped we'd stick with him until he made his decision."

Under the water, I crack my knuckles over and over again as I listen to this story. No wonder Shay is so jaded. After a guy treated them like that, any girl would be fucked up.

"Did you tell him to fuck off?" I ask.

"Oh, yeah." She nods. "I wasn't about to stick with someone who didn't really want me. I would have done anything to be with him, but he wouldn't do anything to be with me. And if he could lie to me for months and months while sleeping with someone else, what else was he capable of?"

"What did the other girl say when he told her?"

"Honestly, I have no idea. I have no clue even who she was. I didn't want to know because honestly, it didn't matter."

"I'm really sorry all of that happened to you, Shay. Nobody should go through that. Sounds like the guy is a total asshole."

"It is what it is. I was young and dumb. I know better now."

"Shay, I get that you got hurt—"

She cuts me off. "Yes, I got hurt. But it took a toll on me that I never could have imagined. Not only did I lose the guy I thought I'd spend my life with, but I also lost all my faith in the opposite sex. He made me feel like I wasn't good enough. I fell down a deep, dark rabbit hole that I wasn't sure I was going to be able to crawl my way out of. I was beyond depressed, drinking constantly. For a while, I honestly didn't know if I was going to make it."

"What changed?" I ask. "How'd you get through it?"

She stares off in the distance and smiles as a memory hits her. "I got a dog."

"Bones, right?"

She nods. "When I'd just about hit rock bottom, I just so happened to hear someone at the bar talking about how they had one Doberman puppy left that no one seemed to want because he was the runt of the litter. They'd had lots of people come look at him, but everyone had passed for one reason or another. I asked to see a picture and immediately fell in love. I picked him up that night, and he's been with me ever since. He's a big baby who whines a lot and is the epitome of a Velcro dog. And he has stomach issues and anxiety, so he's a handful. But one day, I realized that I'd been so busy taking care of him and falling in love with his sweet little face that I wasn't so sad anymore."

"Sounds like he came to you at the perfect time."

"I'm not always one who considers myself religious, but I know that some sort of unseen force brought that dog into my life that day." She takes another drink. "But there you go. You wanted to know why I don't do relationships or things like cuddling. There you have it."

"You know, Shay, not all men are like that. You shouldn't give up on love just because of one bad apple."

"Maybe. But not trying and not getting hurt is a lot less scary than the alternative. It's just easier this way. I've got my house, my job, and my dog. When I want to get laid, I go out and do it. Isn't that why you don't do relationships and why you just try to keep things just casual?"

My face scrunches up. "Is that why you think I'm single? Because I just want to get laid and nothing more?"

"Isn't it?"

"Shay, I'm not opposed to relationships. Hell, I'd love to be in one if I could find the right girl. But I'm not about to waste my time—or hers—if it's not going anywhere. We can just have some fun and call it a day. But I still believe that my dream girl is out there."

She looks up at me. "How will you know when you've found her?"

I think for a moment. "Dan said something today that I think is a good way to look at it. He knew Becky was the one when he realized that his life was so much better with her than without her. With most of the girls I take home, my life will be exactly the same when they leave the next day. When a woman comes along who makes me sure that my life would be worse without her in it, I will do everything in my power to keep her in it."

"I guess I've never thought it about that way, but there's a flaw in your logic."

"What's that?"

"The other person has to feel the same way. You put your heart in their hands and hope that they don't break it. I did feel that way about someone, but it didn't matter."

Pointing at her, I say, "But let me ask you something. Now that you are removed from the situation, don't you think your life is better now? If you and Alan wouldn't have broken up, you never would have gotten Bones."

"Hm. I guess you're right."

I squint my eyes shut as tightly as I can. When Shay asks what the hell I'm doing, I tell her that I'm trying to burn this moment into my brain—the moment when Shay admitted that I'm right about something.

She laughs. "Oh, shut up. Alright, enough of this heavy stuff about me. I'm tired of drudging up bad memories. Let's talk about something else."

"What do you want to talk about?"

She thinks for a moment, leaning back against the tub. Her tits pop out from the top of the water, and I try not to stare. But damn, they look even sexier all wet and soapy.

Taking another drink of tequila, she licks a rogue drop off her bottom lip. "Let's play truth or dare."

I chuckle because Shay could make me *do* anything and *tell* anything just by asking right now. She's naked in a bathtub. If she were to lean forward and touch my cock, I'd probably give her my whole life savings.

"Alright, you ask first," I tell her.

"Truth or dare?"

"Truth," I say.

"Okay, you say you're looking for that perfect girl to come along. What does that entail? What does 'the one' look like for you?"

"Nah, Shay, I don't need perfect. Perfect is no fun. But the *right* girl? That's a different story. Looks wise, I don't have a type."

She interrupts. "I know. I've seen all the women you've taken home from the bar."

"Touche." I laugh. "I just care that we have a good connection. We have to have fun. That was the big piece that was missing with Kyra. I just want someone I can laugh with. Someone I can get excited about accomplishments and celebrate life with. Someone who will have my back while I have hers."

"Fair enough." She looks like she wants to say more, but she doesn't.

"Truth or dare?" I ask.

She shocks the hell out of me when she says, "Truth."

I have no idea what to say because I was convinced she was going to pick dare. There are a million things I want to know about Shay, so it's hard trying to narrow it down to one.

Finally, I settle on, "What did you think about me before this week? I mean, I get that we kind of knew each other, but I'm sure you had preconceived notions about me."

"Man-whore," she replies very seriously before busting out laughing. "I'm just kidding."

"I guess you're not wrong," I say, shrugging my shoulders.

"I thought that you were always fun. I liked that you didn't treat me like a weirdo like some of the other folks in town. When you'd come into the bar, I knew you'd put a smile on my face. But I also thought that there had to be some reason below the surface why every woman in town was so eager to go home with you."

"And what do you think now?" I ask.

"I've seen what that tongue can do, so I totally understand why they went home with you." She giggles.

"You're just so funny tonight, aren't you?" I tease.

She points her finger at me. "Hey, I'm always funny. But now, I think that you're a really sweet guy who has a good heart. Maybe that's another reason all those women are drawn to you. And sir, that was two questions."

"Sorry. Your turn."

"What did you think about me before this week?" She asks.

"You can't just steal my question," I tell her.

"Well, answer it, and I'll ask another one."

"Honestly? I thought you were kind of a hard-ass. You were always witty and sarcastic and never seemed to take shit from anyone." Before she asks the inevitable next question, I decide to go ahead and answer it. "And now, I think that you're more fun than I could have imagined. You have this great personality, and you're not going to change for anyone."

That gets a smile out of her that I haven't seen before. If I didn't know any better, I'd say Shay Baxter may actually be blushing.

"You still have another question," I say.

"Hmm." She thinks for a moment. "Since being here, do you feel any differently about Kyra?"

"Seeing Kyra here makes me wonder how I dated her for as long as I did. I guess when I was in the trenches, it was easy to overlook a lot of the shit she did. Now, I can see exactly who she is."

She nods. "I guess. But you *are* her ex. It's not like you two were likely to be besties."

"No, but we could be civil. She asked me to leave her alone and not to fight for her. That's exactly what I did, and she's pissed about that too. I should have learned a long time ago that there is no making her happy."

"Fair enough. Your turn."

"What's your favorite thing to do in the bedroom?"

"Like sex-wise?"

"Sex, foreplay, whatever."

"Well, like I said before, you going down on me feels pretty incredible. I think that may be my favorite."

That gets me to puff out my chest like you wouldn't believe. To hear that Shay thinks that *my* pussy eating is her favorite thing makes me want to do it to her all night long.

"That's my favorite thing too," I tell her.

She says, "Okay, I have to ask—why do you like going down on girls so much? I'm sure you've heard your nickname around town, Mr. Pussy."

"Yeah, I've heard the nickname, but I try not to let it go to my head. It's just gossip."

She leans forward in the water, looking up at me with her big eyes. "That's what I thought, too—until I experienced it for myself."

Grabbing her chin between my thumb and finger, I say, "You want to know why I like it so much?"

She nods.

"Because there is nothing sexier than knowing I can make you come with just my tongue. I love the way your hands fist in my hair. I can feel the moment when your legs start trembling and your breath hitches in your throat. I love tasting how wet you get and feeling your clit get more sensitive with every passing minute. And when you come, I love feeling your pussy pulse against my tongue. Every move. Every moan. I love it all."

She takes a deep breath as if trying to regain her composure after my little speech. I know she's thinking about it now. She's picturing my head between her legs as my tongue licks her clit until I make her come over and over again.

Under the water, I reach between her legs and lightly rub her pussy lips, prompting her to open for me. When she does, I start to rub. I tell her, "And this pretty little piercing that you have makes eating your pussy that much more fun."

"I don't know that I believe you," she moans. "You may have to prove that to me."

Gladly.

"Come on," I tell her, taking her by the hand and leading her out of the tub. We take a couple minutes to dry off before I take her to the bed.

I lie down, my cock already hard as a rock and standing at attention. "Come here, and sit on my face," I say.

While hooking her leg over my head, she says, "With these thighs and this ass, you may not be able to breathe."

"I'll manage."

She lowers herself onto me, and I push my tongue inside her entrance. I begin teasing her, going just slow enough to drive her insane.

"Devon," she moans. "I need more."

I tell her, "Ride my tongue, Sunshine. Do it exactly how you want it."

I hold my tongue out, flattening it so that she can rub her clit against it at the speed and pressure she wants. She starts slowly, trying to find her rhythm. Once she does, she uses her hips to slide forward and back, grinding against me.

She holds onto the headboard for better leverage while I use my hands to reach up and play with her nipples.

I can't see her face, but I can tell how much she's enjoying it. Everything else she's doing shows me how close she's getting. The way her moans are getting louder. The way her speed increases. The way her body begins to tremble on top of me.

My cock aches, wanting nothing more than to be touched right now.

But it's just going to have to wait. Making Shay come first is more important.

I want to talk to her, to tell her how fucking sexy she is, but I don't dare move my tongue right now. I'm going to stay exactly where I am until she's coming all over my face.

And it doesn't take much longer. Soon enough, she grinds against me all the way to her orgasm. I pinch her nipples as she screams my name.

I'd give anything to make her scream my name all the damn time.

Even after this week is over.

But I try to push those thoughts from my head. I only have enough blood to adequately manage one of my heads at a time, and right now, I'd really like to focus on the one below my belt.

She climbs off my face, and I tell her to lie down.

"No," she argues. "Now, I want to ride something else."

I watch her quickly run over and grab a condom out of my suitcase. I'm sure as shit glad I brought a whole box. Being a horn dog has its advantages.

She comes back and quickly rolls it on over the head. Then, she climbs on board. Watching her ride me is everything. She leans her hands on my chest so that she can push me into her harder and deeper. She switches it up from straight up and down to circling her hips while she does it.

It's hard to hold on while watching her sexy tits bounce up and down and hearing her moan my name.

Shay is wild.

That's the best way I can describe her.

Every time I think I'm starting to keep up with her, she does something else that blows my mind.

Every time I start to crack her code, she changes the password.

But I'm sure as hell going to keep having fun trying.

Chapter Eighteen

SHAY

"Shay, why is this dog so lazy?" Suzie asks, pointing the camera to Bones, who is sprawled out on the couch, half asleep.

"Awww, look at my baby!" I cry.

"But for real, Shay. This dog is a handful. He wakes me up to go outside at five AM, so I let him out. Two minutes later, he's on the other side of the door, whining to come in. I let him in, and he passes back out until ten or eleven. What kind of lifestyle is he living?"

I laugh. "He's living *my* lifestyle. I'm a bartender. I'm not typically up early. I let him out, and he always goes back to bed with me. He's probably offended that you're not snuggling with him."

"Oh, he laid in bed with me last night. I think he will survive." As if suddenly remember something else to tell me, she says, "Oh! And I tried taking him for a walk. Shay, he practically screamed the second we left the driveway. Your neighbors probably thought I was trying to kidnap him."

"He doesn't like leaving the house. Even walks freak him out. He's a homebody."

"Freaking weirdo," she whispers.

"Leave that baby alone."

"Anyway, tell me all about your trip. How's it going with Mr. Pussy? Oh wait, is he there with you?"

"No, he went to go find us some breakfast."

She grins. "Look at him being all sweet."

"Things are fine," I tell her. "Aside from his crazy ex-girlfriend being here, everything is going smoothly."

"Have you...you know?"

"Maybe," I say, trying to contain my smile.

"Oh my gosh! You have! Tell me everything!" She squeals, getting Bones to get off the couch to come over and make sure she's okay.

"Sssh, Bones," she says. "Let's listen to Mom tell us about the man who may be your new daddy."

"Whoa! I think you're getting way too ahead of yourself. Just because I've taken a ride on Mr. Pussy doesn't mean that I'm ready to date the man. A test drive doesn't lock me into buying the car."

"So, you *have* slept with him!"

I sigh and roll my eyes. "Yes, he and I have slept together. Now, can we drop it?"

"For now. But when you get back, I'm going to need a detailed account. Hell, if it sounds good enough, maybe I'll take my own ride."

Something about her words puts me on edge. I'm not sure exactly what it is, but I know I don't like it.

She goes on to say, "But aside from the sex stuff, everything else is going well?"

"Yep," I reply. "Devon's been great. We've actually been having a lot of fun. He makes me laugh."

This time, it's a different type of smile that creeps across her lips. "Why, Miss Baxter, do you like him?"

"That's ridiculous. We are friends. That's it."

"Okay, Shay, whatever you say."

I hear Devon putting his key in the lock. Not wanting him to hear any of this conversation, I say, "Alright, well, Devon's back, so we are going to eat some breakfast. I'll talk to you later."

I shout a quick goodbye to Bones and end the video chat.

Devon walks in with a big silver tray in his hands. "Hey, gorgeous. Everything okay?"

"Yeah, I was just calling to check on Bones."

"How's he doing?"

"Pretty good. He and Suzie are putting up with each other just fine."

Devon walks over to set the tray on the small table before bringing me over one of the plates. Under the silver dome, there's a bagel, some eggs, and fresh fruit.

"This looks delicious," I tell him. "Thank you."

"Of course. Even though everyone is doing their own things this morning, there was still a small little buffet set up for everyone to come and grab what they wanted."

"Man, they've really thought of everything for this week, haven't they?"

"Yeah, I'm sure Becky has been dreaming of this week ever since she was like five." He takes a bite of his eggs. "You ever think you'll get married?"

"That's a loaded question," I mumble. I still can't believe I opened up about as much as I did last night. I rarely tell anyone about Alan, and I'm not sure what makes Devon so special.

It was probably just the tequila.

At least that's what I'm telling myself.

Devon says, "You don't have to tell me if you don't want to."

"No, it's alright." I think for a second. "I don't know if I'll get married. I guess that would require me letting someone in enough to even get close. I'm not opposed to it, but I don't know that it's number one on my to-do list. Marriage is essentially just a piece of paper. It's the commitment that matters. What about you? Do you want to get married?"

"Well, Shay, I mean, it's a bit sudden, but if you're asking—"

"Ha. Ha. Ha." I put emphasis on each word. "You couldn't handle me as a wife."

"Sweetheart, I *could* and *would* handle you every damn night."

His words get me all tingly, but I try not to focus on them. "Answer my question, Cassanova."

"Uh, yeah, sure. I guess marriage could be a thing I see myself doing. Maybe. I'm with you. To me, it's just a piece of paper. I think if two people love each other enough, they don't *need* to get married. Lord knows I watched my momma walk down the aisle enough times to know that marriage isn't always forever."

I know Devon's brothers because they come into the bar with him every couple of weeks, but I haven't heard him talk about his mom much. Since I didn't grow up in Maple Oaks, I don't know all of the sordid details of the local townsfolk.

"Tell me about your mom," I prompt.

"Tammy Samson is a character," he says. "One who's always been unlucky in love. Our whole lives she was searching for Mr. Right but ended up finding all the Mr. Wrongs. She was with every guy who would have her. She let some of them play daddy, but they were usually gone pretty quick. It wasn't that she was a bad mom, but I don't think she was necessarily present all the time."

"Did she ever actually meet Mr. Right?" I ask.

"Well, she's married if that's what you're asking." He laughs. "Rob seems like a good guy, though. They seem pretty solid. Knock on wood. What about you? What was it like growing up with two dads?"

"School was hard because of all the dirty looks, and some people were straight up assholes. But besides that, I loved it. Then again, I've never known anything different."

"Feel free not to answer this if you don't want to, but were you adopted, or did you come from a surrogate?"

"Surrogate," I reply, taking another bite. "Both of my dads used their *samples,* so they technically don't know which one of them is my biological dad, but one of them is."

"Did they have any more kids?"

"Nope. They got it perfect on the first try," I tease.

He smiles. "They sure did."

Not wanting things to get too heavy, I ask, "What is on the plan for today? More wedding festivities?"

"Not until tonight. We've got the bachelor and bachelorette parties. But until then, we are free to do whatever we want."

"Do you have anything in mind?"

"Actually, I think I do."

"This is gorgeous," I tell Devon as my eyes gaze around the spot that we spent the past hour walking to.

Nestled in an enclave of old trees sits a small lake. Lily pads are scattered around the outside, and wildflowers randomly grow throughout the grass. There's a dock on one end with an old rowboat. Willow trees hang over the water with butterflies flying around them. It looks like a scene that would be on a jigsaw puzzle.

"How the hell did you find this place?" I ask.

"I got on Google to see if anything was remotely around us and came up empty, but a few people talked about the pond in their reviews of the resort."

Holding my hand, he leads me onto the deck where we follow it out into the water. We take a seat on the end, letting our feet dangle. I quickly take my shoes off to let my toes kiss the water.

Devon says, "I figured we could get out of the room and still have some alone time."

Leaning my head on his shoulder, I reply, "It's perfect."

As we sit here, listening to the soft hum of the bugs who call the lake home, I take a moment to reflect on the past few days. When I agreed to come on this trip with Devon, I never thought that buried under this notorious ladies' man would be someone so sweet and compassionate.

I figured I may get a few good orgasms out of this trip, but I had no idea I'd be gaining a really good friend.

Is that all we are? Friends?

I guess so because that's all I'm willing to give.

Devon says, "Why don't you tell me what's going on in that big, beautiful brain of yours?"

I try to think of something to say because I really don't want to tell the truth. "Just thinking of how amazing this place is."

"Yeah, it really is." He kisses the top of my head. "But why don't you tell me what you're really thinking about?"

Fuck.

151

I hesitate for a moment before replying, "Just thinking how it's been a really great week so far."

I could have given some smartass or sarcastic answer, but now doesn't seem like the time. This moment is too great to ruin with my dark sense of humor. And I really do want him to know that I'm enjoying myself.

He leans down to press a kiss to my lips. We've kissed a lot over the past few days, but this one feels different.

With this one, it's not a precursor to sex.

And no one is watching.

It's a private moment between just the two of us.

Yes, this one is different.

Because unlike before, where our kisses usually open the floodgates of my vagina, this one seems to have a different effect.

This one seems to tug on my heart strings.

And I'm not quite sure how I feel about that.

Chapter Nineteen

SHAY

"Why is your penis bigger than mine?" Shelly asks me, holding up her cock-shaped necklace.

I look back and forth between the two of us. "Are you jealous?" I ask.

"Kind of. I want a bigger dick."

An already tipsy Becky cackles. "Ha! That's what she said!"

I like drunk Becky.

"How do I get a bigger one?" Shelly asks.

I reply. "You can't. You have to have some of that big dick energy."

She starts to pout when Wendy interrupts us. "Calm down. All the penis necklaces are the same size."

Becky practically shouts, "Prove it! Lay them on the table and measure!"

So far, the bachelorette party is going better than expected. You'd think wearing light-up penis necklaces, crowns, and shiny pink sashes would be awkward to wear in public.

And maybe it would be if we were anywhere but a drag show.

Here, we seem to fit in rather nicely.

Our server, who is dressed up like Whitney Houston, brings us another round.

Shelly points to her necklace and asks, "Excuse me, Miss Houston, who do you think has the bigger penis?"

"Oh, honey, if you think that's big, we need to get you with some better dick."

We all laugh and then, I ask if we can have some appetizers. Whitney hands me a menu, and I order one of everything for us all to share. I'll pay for the food if I have to, but as I watch all these women throw back the drinks, I know I need to get something in their stomachs besides alcohol. Otherwise, this bachelorette party will be over before it really starts.

Thankfully, it doesn't take long for us to have a wide assortment of plates laid out in front of us. Everyone digs in and seems to gain at least a little of their composure back.

Thank God. I get enough of handling sloppy drunks at work. I don't really want to do it now.

The drag show starts, and we get riveting performances from lookalikes of Cher, Reba, Dolly, and even Adele. They're all wonderful, making the crowd go wild.

I'm no stranger to drag shows. Having two gay dads made sure of that. It's where we spent my 21st birthday. Hell, Dad was even a performer back before he met Pops.

I wasn't looking forward to being here with all these women who I still don't really know...and Kyra, who I really can't stand. But being here feels a little like a piece of home.

And as for Kyra, she's been quiet. All of her attention seems to be focused on her phone. Her thumbs move at the speed of light as she sends text after text. By the way steam is practically pouring out of her ears, I'm guessing she and Chad are fighting.

Part of me wonders what about.

But a bigger part of me doesn't care. She's probably giving Chad the same shit she used to give Devon.

Speaking of Devon...

I pull out my phone to send him a text just to see what the guys are up to, but when I look, I see he's already beat me to it.

Devon: Man, I wish you and I were still alone in our room together.

My thumbs type out a reply.

Me: What would we be doing?

Three little dots appear for what seems like forever. And I know this is going to be good.

With Devon's dirty mouth, I would expect nothing less. I've always been a talker during sex, but a lot of the men I've been with haven't been or aren't very good at it.

Devon, on the other hand, can add it to the long list of things he's incredible at.

Finally, a text pops through.

Devon: If you and I were alone right now, I would've already made you come with my tongue at least twice before burying my cock deep inside you. I'd be bending you over, fucking you doggy, getting you close and then pulling out to finish you with my fingers while you squirt all over my hand.

Lord.

I type back: **Sounds fun. Want to do it when we get back later tonight?**

Devon: Definitely. I can't stop thinking about your sweet pussy.

Wanting to make sure of that fact, I take the opportunity to sneak off to the restroom long enough to snap a picture of my lady bits. Not wearing panties has its advantages.

I attach the photo to a text message saying: **This pussy?**

Immediately a response comes through.

Devon: Fuck, Shay. Warn me before you do that. These guys are all horny as fuck, and I don't want one of them looking over my shoulder, trying to sneak a peek.

Me: Don't want anyone to see the goods?

Devon: Fuck, no! This week, I want to be the only man seeing/playing with your pussy.

I'm not able to control the smile that spreads across my lips. Thankfully, nobody sees that either.

Before I can respond, another message pops through.

Devon: I feel like a bit of a hypocrite, though. We are at a strip club where all the women have their goodies on full display.

Me: Oh, I bet you're having fun.

Devon: Eh, it's always a little weird going with a bunch of guys. It's awkward knowing your friends are getting boners while getting lap dances.

Me: Are you getting a boner while you have a lap dance?

Devon: Nah. No lap dances. I already have a boner for another reason.

Me: Watching all the sexy pole dancing?

Devon: Nope. My fake girlfriend sent me a picture of her pretty pussy, and now, I can't stop thinking about it.

I don't know if I believe him about not getting a dance. Isn't that the main point of going to a strip club? Getting grinded on by topless women?

I've never cared much if a guy I'm seeing goes to the *gentleman's club*.

They can look. They just can't touch. The touching is saved for me.

Another text comes through.

Devon: Can't wait to see you later.

My corny smile is back, but this time, it doesn't go unnoticed.

Wendy coos, "Looks like someone is texting her man."

"Maybe," I say, trying to go stone-faced once again.

Becky pokes out her bottom lip. "Aw, I miss Daniel."

Wendy asks, "What are the boys up to?"

I don't want to say for fear that some of these women may not know, or like, where their men are.

But Becky doesn't seem to care. "They're at the strip club."

I look over at Kyra, whose nostrils are flaring. Looks like that may be what she and her lovebird were fighting about.

My attention then turns to Wendy. I feel like I know a dirty little secret since Devon told me she was a stripper. There's no way I'm going to tell her I know that information.

Shelly asks Becky, "Don't you care that Dan is at a club like that?"

"No," Becky replies. "Let him have his fun for one more night. In two days, his strip club days will be over."

A moment later, she adds, "But I do miss him. I want to go see him. I wish we could."

"Why can't we?" I ask. "Let's go see what they're doing."

I can't believe I'm suggesting that, but I'm curious. Plus, the next drag show doesn't start for a while, and if we sit here bored, everyone is going to get way too shitfaced.

Drunk Becky jumps right on board. "Fuck, yeah! Let's go see some titties!"

When no one immediately moves, I say, "You heard the bride. Let's go see some titties."

Chapter Twenty

DEVON

"Do you want a dance, sugar?" One of the dancers runs her fingertips along my shoulders as she steps in front of me. She's the fifth one to ask me in the past hour.

"No, thanks," I tell her. "I'm just enjoying the view."

When she walks away, one of the guys asks, "Why aren't you getting a dance, man? I'm sure Shay wouldn't care."

One of the other ones says, "Hell, we saw the dance she started giving you the other night. She could probably give some of these women a run for their money."

A dancer walks by, and he adds, "No offense, sweetheart."

I say, "You're right. My girl is hot as fuck. I'll wait until I can look *and* touch later on tonight."

A moment later, I feel another pair of hands touching my shoulders behind me.

Here we go again.

A sultry voice whispers in my ear, "Hey, stud. You want a dance?"

"No thanks, I'm g—" I stop cold when the woman walks around to my front, and I see it's Shay.

"You sure?" She smiles. "Word on the street is that I'm pretty good at it."

She sways her hips back and forth a little, but before she gets very far, I grab her by the hand and pull her toward me until she's sitting in my lap. Her ass sits on one knee with her legs draped over the other.

I say, "You stay right here. Let them know my lap is reserved for you. What are you doing here?"

She points to the group of women she came in with. "Drunk Becky wanted to come see her man. I guess she missed him."

"Is that right? Because Becky's all talk...unless someone puts an idea in her head. Showing up at a strip club seems like much more of a Shay thing to do."

She chews on the inside of her cheek. "Well, maybe I spurred the idea along."

"Oh, yeah. Did you miss me?"

"Don't get excited," she says. "I just wanted to come see if my pretend boyfriend was behaving himself. And you said you missed my sweet pussy. Figured I'd bring it to you."

I lean in so that I'm not shouting over the music. "My cock has been hard as a rock ever since you sent me that pic."

"Oh, really?" She wiggles her ass a little, rubbing against me.

"Let me just tell you that I'm so fucking glad you forgot underwear this week. In fact, I vote that you never wear them again."

"Oh, I bet you'd love that."

Yes, I would. Then again, after our little fling ends, if I knew she wasn't wearing any panties, and I wasn't the one touching her, it may be pure torture.

We both turn our attention toward Becky, who is giving Dan her own version of a lap dance.

When she stumbles a bit, I ask, "How much has she had to drink?

"A couple of Long Island iced teas."

"Good lord."

A woman on the stage catches Shay's attention. She twists and turns on the pole like her limbs are made of rubber.

Shay turns to me and holds out of her hand. "Give me some cash."

"Why?"

"Because any woman who can do *that* while hanging upside down on a pole deserves to have some cash shoved in her g-string."

I lift her slightly so that I can reach my wallet.

"Man," I begin. "It really *is* like you're my girlfriend. How much do you want?"

I hold open the wallet, and she takes everything out.

"Hey," I say. "That's all my cash."

She points to the dancer. "Can you do that?"

"Not even a little bit."

"Okay, then."

I watch her get up and walk to the edge of the stage. The dancer moves toward her so that Shay can stick the wad of cash in the string of her barely-there panties.

Man, Shay is fucking sexy.

Most women would be offended that their man was at a strip club. Shay is shoving money in a stripper's thong.

But I don't know that it means much. Shay is not really my girlfriend.

I keep telling myself that. But every time I say it, it gets a little harder to swallow.

Letting go of our little fantasy world is going to be more difficult than I imagined.

Shay makes her way back over to me, but before she can say anything, Dan interrupts.

"Hey, we are going to move this party. Becky's clumsy dance broke a few glasses, and we're getting dirty looks from the staff.

Shay and I both ask in unison, "Where are we going?"

"Bowling," I say while tying my rented shoes. "Interesting choice after the strip club."

Dan leans toward me and whispers, "I tried to think of something that would help Beck sober up a bit."

I look at Becky who is headed toward us with two pitchers of beer.

Pointing at her, I ask, "How's that going for you?'

"Well, shiiiiiit."

Shay leans in to whisper, "That one is going to be lucky to be vertical by the end of the night."

"No joke," I agree. "So, are you any good at bowling?"

"Eh, I'm alright."

Dan takes a minute to split us into teams. As if he doesn't realize what he's doing, he puts Shay and I up against Kyra and Chad. I'll have to give him shit for that later.

After we pick out balls and get ready to go, Chad asks, "Do you guys want to make things more interesting?"

"What did you have in mind?" I ask.

He shrugs while pushing his blonde hair out of his face. "Maybe we put fifty bucks on the game."

I open my mouth to politely decline, but Kyra decides to give her two cents that absolutely no one asked for. "Oh, come on, sweetie. We shouldn't take money from the less fortunate. Look at Shay. She clearly needs all the funds she can get."

Now, it's Shay's turn to jump in. "Make it a hundred, and you've got yourself a bet."

"Deal." Chad says with a snarky grin.

I whisper to Shay, "What are you doing?"

"Trust me."

Well, okay then.

Shay's up first. She pauses for a moment, holding the ball in front of her chest before taking her shot.

The ball rolls down the lane with effortless ease. All of us stare intently, waiting to see what happens.

As the ball makes contact with the pins, all ten of them fall down, one right after the next.

Shay turns around as though she's not the least bit surprised as she walks back to the table.

Chad gives a loud laugh, "I think you guys have a ringer!"

The look on Kyra's face is priceless. With her arms crossed over her chest, she looks like a toddler who had her toy taken away. I'm tempted to take a photo just to laugh at later on.

As Kyra stands up to take her turn, Shay sits back down. I brush her hair out of her face and whisper in her ear, "Is there anything you can't do?"

"No," she jokes.

Kyra rolls the ball straight into the gutter.

Twice.

It's the best show of karma I've ever seen.

Chad and I both knock down a decent amount of pins but nothing special.

The rest of the game continues on in exactly the same fashion. Kyra barely hits anything. Chad and I are right in the middle of the road. And Shay picks up either a strike or a spare on each frame.

Thank goodness for her.

When the game is over, and the scores are settled, Chad sets a hundred bucks on the table and asks, "Okay, Shay, how'd you get so good at bowling?"

"My dads were in a league, so we spent a ton of time practicing on the lanes."

Kyra asks, "Dads? As in plural?"

I look at Shay who is cracking her neck. "Yes, Kyra, I have two dads. Before you say anything about that fact, I need you to know that I can take a lot of shit, but if you bring my dads into this, I'll take you to the parking lot and kick your teeth down your throat."

Kyra stares at her, trying to decide if she wants to retreat or charge right into battle.

Before she can make any type of decision, Chad makes it for her. "Sweet cheeks, why don't you go take a walk?"

When she tries to argue, he gives a stern, "Now."

Man, if I would've ever talked to Kyra like that when we were together, she would have picked a fight in front of all these people before ignoring me and denying me sex for a week.

But much to my surprise, with Chad there's no argument. She just gets up and walks away.

"Sorry about her," Chad says. "That one's wound a little tight. Hell, you know. You dated her."

"Yeah," is all I say in return.

He adds, "Later on, I'll talk to her. Tell her to stop acting like a spoiled brat."

Kyra may be exactly that, but I would've never said that to someone while we were dating. You should have your girls back...even when she's being a brat.

Chad's phone rings, and he excuses himself to go answer it.

Shay mumbles, "Kind of late for a phone call."

"Mm-hmm."

"Chad's a Grade A asshole."

"Yep," I agree once again.

"Why do you think she's putting up with it? I can't imagine that she would've put up with that with you."

"There's one thing that Chad has that I don't."

"What's that?" She asks.

"Money."

Shay playfully bumps her shoulder into mine. "I'll take you and your amazing tongue over a bunch of cash any day."

I get that she's joking or being sarcastic or whatever it is that Shay does, but it still makes me smile.

She even goes on to add, "And for the record, your tongue isn't the only thing you have to offer."

That makes me feel even better. I'm well aware of what the women I've been with call me. Do I feel like I'm being used or something? No. It's not like I was ready to jump into anything after Kyra.

But it's good to hear that I'm good for more than just a few orgasms. Or at least Shay thinks I am.

I could lie and say I don't know why her opinion matters to me.

But I do know.

It's because this week, Shay has disproved every preconceived notion I had about her. And after seeing what's underneath her hard outer shell, I like what I'm seeing more and more.

I want to tell her all of this, but for now, I'm keeping my mouth shut. This week is going too well to ruin it.

Instead, I put my arm around Shay's shoulder and give her a kiss on the cheek.

I'm just about to suggest that we duck out of here and spend the rest of the night naked in bed.

But drunk Becky and Dan interrupt us. Dan says, "Come on, Beck wants to go dancing. Let's hit a club."

Shay and I both stammer, trying to think of an excuse as to why we can't go. Unfortunately for us, Dan and Becky won't hear any of it.

Guess we're going dancing.

Chapter Twenty-one

SHAY

"Do you feel like we're too old to be here?" I ask Devon over the loud thumping music.

"Definitely," he shouts back.

Unfortunately, the only places to dance that were remotely close to the bowling alley were a couple of clubs near the local community college—meaning most of the patrons are college students.

Just over thirty doesn't seem that old, except when you're around kids who are still students. A few of them look at us like we're aliens who just crash landed on their planet.

But Becky is so drunk she doesn't even seem to notice. She's just buying round after round of shots for everyone.

I try to tell her that all the liquor she's mixed together likely isn't going to end well, but she doesn't want to listen.

Tomorrow's going to suck for her.

After throwing back a shot of vodka, Becky asks, "Who wants to come dance with me?"

Everyone sits quietly at our large corner table, avoiding all eye contact with the bride. At this point, I think everyone is just ready to be done.

But Becky's not.

And unluckily for me, she grabs my hands announcing, "Come on, Shay! Come dance with me!"

"No, really, I'm okay," I try to protest.

"Nope. You have to. I'm the bride."

Man, she's milking that for all it's worth.

She yanks so hard she about pulls my arm out of its socket. Once I'm on my feet, I follow her to the dance floor.

Neon spotlights frantically shine everywhere as the heavy beat of the music practically vibrates through the whole building.

We start to move, and Becky throws any inhibitions she has left straight out the window by grinding on me.

She slurs, "If no one wants to join us, let's give them a good show."

I follow her lead and do her sexy dance. I'm all about getting dirty and sweaty, dancing at a club.

It's just usually with a guy.

But whatever the bride wants, I guess.

Occasionally, my eyes catch Devon's, who is staring at me like I'm Little Red Riding Hood, and he's the Big Bad Wolf, ready to devour me.

For him, and him alone, I put on a good show—giving him something to look forward to later.

Becky tries to get someone's attention to bring us more drinks. I use the free moment to continue dancing for Devon. But when I look back, he's no longer at the table.

Hm. Maybe he went to the bathroom or something.

I feel a couple of hands wrap around my hips from behind which triggers my big, goofy smile. It takes me all of about two seconds, though, to realize it's not Devon.

I whip around to see some strange guy with blonde hair and a baby face standing there. Even with taking a step back, I can still smell the liquor on his breath.

"Hey, good looking," he says. "I like the way you move. Want to keep dancing?"

Not with you.

"Listen, buddy, no offense, but you're way out of your element."

"What do you mean?" he asks in drunken confusion.

Patting him on the shoulder, I reply, "You couldn't handle me."

A flash of disappointment flashes across his face. I hope that we're done, but he's not ready to give up.

He grabs my hand and yanks me toward him before palming a handful of my ass.

"Listen, bubba," I start.

Before I can say another word, another large body steps behind me. This time, I recognize it immediately.

Devon.

His deep voice says, "She's spoken for."

"The way she was dancing didn't look like she was spoken for."

"She can dance any way she wants to. Doesn't give you the right to touch her however the fuck you want."

Before walking off, he says, "You really shouldn't leave your girl alone. Might not work out too well."

Once he's out of earshot, I mumble, "What a creep."

Devon asks, "Are you okay?"

Turning around to face him, I wrap my arms around his neck, "I am now."

I press my lips to his, letting our tongues dance while our bodies do the same. Devon's hands grip my hips and pull me close so I'm grinding against him. I can feel his cock that's already half-hard through his jeans.

"Is that a bottle in your pants, or are you just happy to see me?" I joke.

"Oh, it's all you and your sexy dancing."

I reply, "I'm not nearly as good as the women at the strip club."

He leans close to talk in my ear. "You sat on my lap at the strip club. You tell me if my dick was as hard as it is right now."

My eyes flick down to the bulge. "What do you want to do about it?"

"Get your ass in the bathroom," he growls.

"Bathroom?" I ask, confused.

"Unless you'd rather me shove my fingers in your pussy right here on the dance floor."

I don't say a word but instead head straight where Devon commanded.

On the way, I pass Becky, who asks where I'm going. Luckily, she doesn't see Devon slip past me right into the women's restroom.

"I just have to pee," I tell her. "I'll be back. Go see what Dan's doing."

When I manage to get away, I walk into the bathroom. There's a long row of stalls, and I try to look for Devon without being obvious. Under the small walls, I spot his boots in one of the larger stalls all the way at the end.

He must also recognize my shoes because he swings the door open when I reach him. I notice him wiping his hands on a paper towel.

"What are you doing?" I ask.

"I washed my hands. Wasn't about to touch your lady bits with the germs from everywhere we've been tonight."

"How is it that someone so dirty is also so thoughtful?" I tease.

"It's a fine line."

We stare at each other for a split second before throwing the small talk out the window and trapping each other in a passionate kiss. Our hands roam all over the other.

Before I can get too comfortable, he turns me around so my back is pressed against his chest. He kisses the back of my neck while his hands reach into my lowcut shirt and tease my nipples. My head falls back against his chest as I try not to focus on the way my clit pulses, aching to be touched.

I rub my ass against his hard cock, which seems to snap something inside him.

"Hands on the wall," Devon commands.

I do as he says, making sure to stick my backside out to give him a good view. Cool air hits my ass cheeks as he hikes up my dress.

His fingers lightly rub up my thighs before finding my entrance. He teases for a moment.

"Already so wet," he whispers. "I fucking love that you forgot all your panties at home."

Trying to keep my moans quiet as he rubs my clit, I just nod.

It gets a lot harder to keep quiet when I feel two of his fingers slip inside. I inhale a sharp breath, preparing for what's about to come.

It's me.

I'm about to come.

I already know.

When he starts expertly moving his fingers, he slaps his other hand over my mouth to keep me quiet because with the way he's touching that magical spot, I want to scream at the top of my lungs.

Just when I begin to feel my core tighten, and my pussy ready to explode, we hear Becky burst into the bathroom.

"Shay?" She calls. "Shay, I lost our table. And I don't feel so good."

"Becky, you didn't find Dan?" I ask.

"No, I think he left me." Her voice cracks like she's near tears.

Devon pulls his fingers out of me, and I readjust my dress. As much as I'd love to come right now, we both know it's not happening.

I tell him to slip away while I deal with Becky. The moment I exit the stall, I see Becky run into one of her own. She leaves the door open as she starts heaving.

Great.

I really don't want to deal with this, but there's quite literally no one else to help.

Well, besides Dev.

But he's not even supposed to be in here.

As she starts puking her guts out, I hold her hair back and rub her shoulder.

"Am I dying?" She asks between heaves.

"Not today, dear. But it's going to feel like it for a while."

When she takes a break, she flushes and looks up at me. "You're a really good person, Shay. I can see why Devon loves you so much."

The words hit me like a gut punch.

She's the second person to use the L word this week.

This whole thing is supposed to be pretend. I get that maybe we've been doing some good acting, but no one has mentioned the word love at all.

Becky continues, "I thought you two were full of shit, but I see it now. I see the way he looks at you."

"He's not in love with me," I mumble, knowing Becky won't remember any of this tomorrow.

"Oh, yes he does. He's crazy about you. I've never seen him so happy. Let's just say he never once looked at Kyra the way he looks at you."

There's no way. This whole thing is just an act, and in a couple of days, it'll be over.

Period.

I have no idea how long we're in there before I get Becky stable enough to move off the bathroom floor.

When we come out, I'm grateful that Dan and Devon are both waiting outside the bathroom. I hand Becky off to her fiancé before Devon wraps me in a hug.

"Are you okay?" He asks.

"Can we go back to our room?" I'm ready to call this a night.

"I thought you'd never ask."

"Come on. I called us a ride so we wouldn't have to wait around."

"Shit. I forgot my wallet back at the table," I mutter.

"Go on outside. I'll run and grab it and meet you there."

I walk outside and inhale deeply. It's the first time that even a hint of Autumn has been in the air. In Texas, cooler weather is hard to come by.

I move out of the way of the entrance as I wait for Devon.

Pulling out my phone, I decide to send a text to Suzie to see how Bones is doing.

But before I get a chance, the handsy drunk guy from earlier shows back up.

"Hey, sexy."

Great. We've moved from good looking to sexy.

I eye the beer in his hand and can't believe the bartender is still serving him. I would have cut this asshole off a long time ago.

"Oh, you again," I groan.

"I had a feeling you'd ditch that boyfriend of yours."

"I didn't—"

Before I can utter another word, the guy has me pinned against the wall, trying to shove his tongue in my mouth. I raise my hands to push him off me.

But Devon beats me to it. He yanks the guy back so hard that the drunk has trouble keeping his balance.

"Didn't I tell you she was taken?" Devon barks.

"Just look at her. She was practically begging for it."

I barely process what the asshole said before I see Devon's fist swing back before lunging to connect with the guy's face.

"Stay the fuck away from my girl."

Devon takes me by the hand and walks me down the sidewalk to where our ride is waiting. He opens the door for me, and I slide inside.

He holds me close, but neither of us immediately say anything.

I've never seen Devon get upset like that before. In fact, I've never had someone stand up for me like that either. Alan was never the jealous type, and no one else has been serious enough to get to that point.

I'm not one who considers myself in need of saving. I've always handled myself just fine. But something about Devon going all primal caveman is surprisingly hot.

A tiny voice in my head nags that he only did it to make this thing look more believable.

Or maybe he was just being a good guy.

Either way, it's not anything more.

While that may be true, I can't help how good it makes me feel.

And shortly, when we are alone, I plan to return the favor.

Chapter Twenty-two

DEVON

I can't tell you the last time I hauled off and punched someone. It's been years. Hell, it was probably high school when somebody was talking shit about my mom.

I guess I don't like anyone implying certain things about the women in my life. The funny thing is that I never got this bent out of shape over Kyra.

Maybe that should tell me something.

As much as I hate to believe it, I think Shay means more to me than I'm willing to admit.

But I have no idea how Shay feels about any of this because she hasn't said a word to me the entire ride. My fake girlfriend is wildly independent, and I stepped in and acted like a complete brute.

I didn't mean to make her upset or make her feel like she wasn't able to handle herself.

But I just saw red when the guy was running his mouth about her.

Fuck.

When we finally get back to the resort, we walk to our room still in silence. I decide to take my chances and reach down to hold her hand in mine. She doesn't pull away, so I guess that's a good sign.

This feels nice. Right now, we have no one we are trying to impress or convince like we have for the whole week.

But this time seems to feel more *right* than any of those other times. The moment we get through the door, I start talking. "Look, Shay, I'm really sorry. I didn't mean—"

My words are cut off when she kisses me. Her hands waste no time in working on getting us both undressed. I haven't been able to stop thinking about fucking her all night long, but right now, I feel like maybe we should talk about this a little more.

I tangle my fingers in her hair and gently pull her back so I can look at her.

"I need to make sure you're okay," I say.

"When will you realize I'm always okay?" She asks.

"Shay..."

She gives me a sexy smile. "I'm more than okay."

"You're not mad at me?"

"You stood up for me. Why would that make me mad?"

"Because I acted like an overprotective brute."

Another smile. "I kind of liked it."

She leans in to kiss me again, but we aren't done.

"Are you sure?"

"Devon, I've never had anyone do that for me before. I know I can handle myself, but it's nice that for once, I didn't have to. Now, I'm trying to show my appreciation by playing with your cock. Can I do that?"

It's my turn to smile. "Well, since you asked so nicely."

I watch as Shay sinks to her knees before undoing my zipper and pulling out my dick. I'm not completely hard, but she sucks me down her throat anyway.

As I harden inside her mouth, my eyes stay fixed on her. I can't seem to look away. The way she stares up at me as she drags my cock in and out is fucking perfect.

"Damn, girl," I whisper. "You are so fucking sexy. I love the way you suck that dick."

She moans in response, sending vibrations all the way down to my balls. I find myself struggling to hold on, and every time my head touches the back of her throat, the struggle gets more and more difficult.

Finally, I can't take anymore. Grabbing her hair, I say, "I *need* to fuck you."

I pull her to her feet, and in a blur, we strip off each other's clothes. Shay quickly grabs a condom and rolls it on before pushing me onto the bed and climbing on top. This time, she straddles me backwards, giving me a perfect view of her juicy ass. And I don't miss a single moment of watching her slide her pussy onto me. She moves slowly, gently stretching so she can fit it all.

As soon as I'm buried to my balls, that's where the *slow* stops.

With her hands on my thighs, she starts bouncing up and down. I prop a pillow behind my head so that I can get the perfect view of her ass jiggling with every movement. When she starts circling her hips as she rides me, I about lose my damn mind.

Not to blow my own horn, but I usually have no issue going for a marathon session in the bedroom. Shay pushes my limits, though. I feel like I'm constantly on the brink of blowing my load.

"Fuck, Shay," I growl, gritting my teeth and attempting to hold onto any shred of self-control I have left.

She suddenly slows her moves so that she's teasing me by raising up as far as she can while keeping me inside before sinking back down. She throws her head back and moans my name, and I realize I have no control. It's all Shay.

As much as I'd love to keep this going just like this until I fill the condom, that's not happening until I make her come. There's no way in hell I'm about to leave her hanging.

Grabbing her by the hips, I say, "Bring this sexy ass up here."

She slowly backs up until she's hovering over my face.

I pull her down while commanding, "Sit."

She does, and I waste no time in starting to give all my attention to eating her pussy. I do everything I've learned that she likes. Her moans get louder, and I know she's getting closer.

She shifts her position, though, so that her body is draped across mine, and her mouth is level with my dick.

She pulls the condom off and takes me down her throat once more. We stay locked in this position for what feels like forever. She sucks my cock while I lick her clit and play with her piercing.

I make her come twice—each time, giving soft kisses to her pussy until she calms down enough to take some more. When I'm just about to dive in for round three, she starts sucking my dick like a fucking porn star. The woman could suck a golf ball through a damn garden hose.

It takes less than a minute before I can't take anymore. "Holy shit, Shay. I'm going to come."

She keeps going, and my balls tighten as I fill her mouth.

After she swallows and climbs off me, I say, "Damn, woman. I think you're trying to kill me. That was amazing."

She lays down next to me. "Yeah, I have to say that I don't know what I'm going to do without that tongue when this whole thing is over."

I'm beginning to wonder what I'm going to do without *Shay* in general when this whole thing is over.

Chapter Twenty-three

SHAY

D evon hands me a bottle of water from the mini-fridge as I lie in a sleepy heap on the bed.

"You were really great dealing with Becky tonight," he tells me.

"Well, dealing with drunks is part of my job description."

"Still, you were great with handling everything tonight. I feel like you've really been put through the ringer this week."

He sits next to me, and I look up at him. He's still naked, and his hair is all messed up from our dirty activities. He looks so delicious that I'm tempted to get him going all over and over again.

It's official.

Devon Samson has turned me into a horndog.

I wonder exactly how many more orgasms he could give me before I can't take anymore. It sure as hell would be fun to find out.

But every time I hype myself up to move, exhaustion holds me firmly in place.

Devon turns on the TV and flips through channels until he lands on one of those shows that's just a bunch of internet videos of people doing stupid stuff. I let out a cackle at one of a guy who knocks himself in the balls with a wiffle ball bat.

Devon asks, "Before you build your little pillow wall, do you want to snuggle up and watch some TV?"

I should tell him no. The whole thing seems way too intimate. But right now, I don't care. After the chaos of tonight, all I really want is for him to hold me.

We get comfortable—I lie my head on Devon's chest while he runs his fingers through my hair.

The two of us laugh and joke about what's on the show, and meanwhile, I try to ignore how good this feels.

I like my life. Love it, in fact. Most days, I like that I live alone and have no one to answer to. I live my life on my own terms. But moments like these remind me of how lonely I can get. I can't remember the last time I just laid with someone.

Mind you, I don't think the benefits of having a snuggle buddy outweigh the risks of having a broken heart. Besides, I have my dog to snuggle with.

But for tonight—just for tonight—I'll enjoy this. We can play pretend just a little longer despite no one watching.

Devon catches me off guard when he asks, "So, what happens after this week?"

I think for a moment, trying to figure out how I want to answer this. I guess there's really only way to, though.

"We go back to our lives. I go back to slinging drinks and hanging with my dog, and you can get back to adding notches to your bed post." That last part comes out a little snarkier than I intend, but Devon doesn't seem to take offense.

He says, "Luckily, Dan and Becky are going to be on their honeymoon for a couple of weeks. By the time they get back, maybe I'll have come up with an excuse of why we broke up."

"What do you think you'll tell them?" I ask.

"Oh, definitely that you broke up with me."

"Why me?" I shriek.

"Come on, Shay. That's the only way anyone would believe it. You're way too good for me."

"Not true at all," I argue. "You're a great guy."

"Well, thanks," he says with a kiss to the top of my head.

"You could say you got bored with me."

"Are you kidding? No one would buy that. You're the most interesting person at this whole damn wedding. And everyone loves you."

"Everyone except Kyra." I laugh.

"Fuck Kyra."

I look up at him. "Speaking of that, how did you fuck Kyra? I'd imagine that huge stick up her ass made it difficult."

His chest rumbles as he laughs.

"It was decent in the beginning, and surprisingly, she could be wild when she wanted to. But clearly, she was just biding time with me until she found someone better."

I mumble, "I bet she's kicking herself for thinking that guy was Chad. A hundred bucks says his tongue can't do what yours can."

"Honestly, Kyra didn't like it when I went down on her. Saliva grossed her out or something."

"Excuse me?" I ask. "Man, she was missing out. Then again, maybe I should send her a thank you card. If she hadn't been so dumb, you wouldn't have gotten to share that wonderful gift with the world."

"Has anyone told you how dramatic you are?" He teases.

"Never," I quip in response. "So, why are you going to say that I broke up with you?"

"No idea. Maybe that you said you just didn't want a relationship or something."

"Would they believe you cheated?"

"Fuck no."

"Oh?" I ask.

"Look, Shay, like I told you before, I may have a reputation, but I can assure you it doesn't involve cheating. I saw my momma get cheated on way too many times. I'd never do that to a woman."

I can tell I struck a nerve, so I grab him by the chin and turn him to look at me. "Hey, I'm sorry. I was just fucking around. I didn't mean to make you upset."

He smiles. "You didn't. Just telling you why Dan and Becky wouldn't believe I cheated."

I look at him.

Really look at him.

It's hard to believe that this beautiful guy who I used to regard as nothing more than a ladies man has so many layers to him. I had no idea how sweet and genuine he was underneath it all.

Devon Samson has a heart of gold buried within that nice hard chest of his.

Someday, he's going to make some woman extremely happy.

It won't be me.

But somebody else for sure.

"There is always one other option," Devon says.

"What's that?"

He looks down at me. "I tell everyone you were eaten by a shark."

Sighing, I ask, "What's with you and the damn sharks?"

Chapter Twenty-four

DEVON

"**D**amn, woman! Look at you!" I tell Shay as I grab her hand and twirl her in a circle.

"You like?" She asks. "Is it too much?"

I look her up and down once again. The black dress she wears hangs down to just above her knees and clings to every curve. It has long sleeves but is still low cut enough to get a good view of her tits. Her hair hangs in loose waves, and her big eyes have some dark gray makeup on them.

"No. Not too much," I tell her. "You look stunning."

She adjusts the collar on my shirt. "You don't look half bad yourself, Mr. Samson."

The rehearsal dinner tonight is a little fancier than anything else this week, so I thought I better try to look half-decent.

We've spent most of our day in bed.

Eat.

Fuck.

Sleep. Repeat.

We've been trapped in our little bubble, and I've loved every second. Neither of us wanted to get ready to go to this dinner.

I'm grateful, though, that more family and friends will be there tonight. Maybe it'll distract the bride and groom enough for us to sneak away early.

I know that our time left together is limited, and I want to make the most of it. I'd prefer to do that without an audience.

Pulling her close, I say, "In fact, you look so good that I'm going to eat dinner as quickly as possible to get back here and eat *you*."

"Cassanova, if you keep talking like that, we won't make it to the dinner at all."

I use my thumb to run over her bottom lip. "Do you know how hard it's going to be to keep my hands off of you?"

"Who says I want you to do that?" She asks before sucking my thumb into her mouth.

When she releases me, I say, "Well, that will ensure my cock will be hard all fucking night."

"Good. It'll get you all revved up for when we get back."

I hate to break it to her, but I'm revved up around her no matter what.

We finally manage to push our libidos to the back burner and leave the room and head to where the rehearsal dinner is being held.

Instead of just one long table set up, there's now an abundance of small tables set up around the area that are filled with friends and extended family.

We take our seats with the rest of the wedding party and order a couple drinks from a passing waiter.

Kyra and Chad sit a few seats down from us. Chad is non-stop texting while Kyra is chugging champaign like it's going out of style.

The two of them really are a match made in heaven. They're perfect for each other. I hope he's rich enough to make up for the fact that he's an asshole.

As our salads are being served, Shelly shows up, throwing herself in one of the empty seats across from us.

"Sorry, I'm late."

I say, "You didn't miss much. Are you still here alone?"

"Yeah, my husband is on his way. He took a wrong turn, so I was trying to give him directions. I don't want him googling and driving."

I just nod since my brain ceases to work when Shay starts teasing me under the table.

Oh, she's going to pay for that later.

Shelly starts talking again. "Looks like the bride has recovered nicely from her wild night out."

We all turn to look at Becky who is smiling and laughing like eighteen hours ago, she wasn't hugging the porcelain throne.

"Guess so," Shay says. "So, what do you do for a living, Shelly?"

"I'm a teacher. Kindergarten teacher."

"Whoa, you must have the patience of a saint."

Shelly shrugs. "Eh, it helps when you have your own kids, too, I guess."

The two of them make a little more small talk before Shelly's phone vibrates.

"Oh, my hubby's here. I'm going to go grab him. Be right back."

Shay continues teasing me while the next course is being served.

"You're killing me," I tell her. "You know that?"

"Mm-hmm."

Just loud enough for only her to hear, I say, "Your pussy is *mine* later."

"Oh, yeah?"

"I'm going to make you come so hard that you forget your fucking name."

"Are you really trying to get me to stop, or do you want me to tease you more?"

"I think you already know the answer to that, Sunshine."

I go to say something else to her, but when I see the look on her face, I stop.

Her mouth hangs open, and her eyes are wide as saucers.

"Shay?" I ask but get no response.

My gaze follows hers and lands on Shelly and who I'm guessing is her husband—although he looks like he's a good ten-fifteen years older than her.

Shay stares at him in complete disbelief.

I nudge her but still get nothing. When she finally does speak, she says only one word.

But with that one word, everything changes in the blink of an eye.

"Alan?"

Chapter Twenty-five

SHAY

There's no fucking way this is happening.

No way in hell.

Does the universe really hate me that much? Or have I done something to piss God off?

They say it's a small world, but you don't truly fathom how small until you're at a wedding where you know absolutely no one except for your ex-boyfriend and your pretend one.

I look up at Alan. His hair that hangs to his shoulders is pulled back into a ponytail. He still looks the same except that now the dark blonde is layered with a few grays here and there. And he's grown out his facial hair. It used to be just some stubble but has turned into a full beard.

"Hello, Shay," he says with a warm smile.

Well, I guess he would consider it warm. For me, it does nothing but make my skin crawl. That smile used to be able to get me to do anything. Now, all it makes me want to do is punch him in the mouth.

I feel Devon squeeze my hand under the table, reminding me that he's there.

Shelly looks back and forth between Alan and me and asks, "How do you two know each other?"

"Uhh," I begin, not sure exactly what to say.

Apparently, Alan already has his answer already lined up because he replies, "Shay used to be a student of mine."

Oh, that's what we're going with? Just a student?
Can this situation get any worse?

As if a lightbulb goes on in Shelly's head, she says, "Oh my gosh! You're Shay?! *The* Shay!"

What the hell does that mean?

Before I can ask that question out loud, Shelly continues, "Al told me all about you! He said you were one of his favorite students. You used to have the biggest crush on him!"

Huh?

"I remember when I found all those messages on his phone, and he told me that you were another one of his students who were a little boy crazy over him."

It all starts to make sense.

Shelly isn't just the wife of my ex. She was the other woman.

Or the first woman while I was the other.

I don't know.

I had no idea she was another student. He never shared that little tidbit of information.

What he *did* share with me was that he came clean to her. He said that he told her the same thing he told me.

He lied.

He didn't tell her shit except that I was some...crazed fan?

I can only imagine how he talked his way out of trouble when she read the texts between the two of us. He probably deleted one side of the conversation to fit his narrative.

Shelly says, "What a small world!"

"Getting smaller by the minute," I mumble.

Devon turns his head to look at something behind me and whispers, "Are you okay?'

Gritting my teeth, I give a small nod.

As much as I want to spill my guts about Alan to his wife, I catch a glimpse of Becky as I start to open my mouth. She looks so happy—a truly blushing bride.

Despite my disdain for most people, over the past week, I've come to actually like Becky. I'm not going to do anything at her wedding that will cause a scene. I don't want to draw attention away from her.

This isn't my day.

It's hers.

But I need a minute.

"Will you all excuse me?" I ask. "I need to use the restroom before the next course is served."

I quickly get up and walk to the family bathroom. Once inside, I lock the door behind me and try to catch my breath. But that's difficult when it feels like there's an anvil sitting on my chest.

I take a few deep breaths, but no matter how much I try, I can't seem to calm down.

Moments later, there's a knock on the door. I try to call out to say it's occupied, but I can't seem to speak through the wheezing that's now occurring.

"Shay, it's me," Devon says. "Open the door."

I walk over to unlock it and let him in. Once inside, he says, "Holy shit, are you okay?"

When he realizes that I'm not able to breathe, he takes my hands, walking me over to sit on the toilet. "Shit, you're having a panic attack."

He knees in front of me. "Shay, look at me. I need you to breathe with me."

He starts taking slow, deep breaths. When I'm still hyperventilating, he takes my hand and sets it on his chest.

"Feel. Feel my chest and try to make yours mimic mine."

I go to look away, but he says, "Look at me, baby. Just look at me and breathe."

I do what he says, looking into those pretty blue eyes of his. I'm still silently freaking out, wondering if this is going to be the thing that takes me out. But without even realizing it, I have slowed my breathing to match Devon's.

"That's it, baby. Just breathe. I'm here."

When I'm finally calm enough to speak, I say, "He lied. He lied about everything."

"I know," Devon replies. "I'm so sorry."

"I wasn't obsessed with him," I say. "I wasn't some sort of crazed student."

"I never believed a word of that bullshit."

"Shelly's the other girl he was sleeping with. He said he told her everything."

"He's a fucking asshole."

I just nod.

"Are you okay?" Devon asks.

When I look at him, he says, "Yeah, yeah. I know that Shay Baxter is always okay. But I need to know if you're *okay.*"

That's a loaded question.

Am I okay?

I have no idea.

But I do know one thing.

"I'm pissed," I reply. And it's the truth. I can feel the blood pumping through my veins as the events of the past few minutes flash through my head on repeat.

Much to my surprise, he smiles. "That's my girl. Do you want to skip the rest of dinner and go back to the room? I can make up an excuse."

"No, it's alright. Tonight isn't about me. It's about Becky and Dan. Let's just go back and try to keep to ourselves."

"Okay, but you tell me if you want to leave. One word, and we are gone. Promise you'll tell me if it becomes too much?"

I nod. "Sure."

"Shay, I'm serious. Promise?"

"Okay, I wasn't serious before, but I am now. I'll tell you if I want to leave. But it may seem pretty obvious if I'm like *hey, let's go.* I don't want to give that jerk the satisfaction of knowing he made me run away."

"Hm. We need a code word." He thinks for a minute. "You say the word *shark,* and we are gone."

"Devon, was Shark Week on TV before we left home or something?"

He points at me. "Shark. Got it?"

"Got it."

When we get back to the table, the entrees have been served, and everyone seems to be in their own little world.

Thank goodness.

I could use a reprieve.

Unfortunately, I don't think I'm going to get it.

Shelly asks, "Are you okay, Shay? You were gone a minute."

"I'm fine. There was a line at the restroom."

She then asks, "So, what did you think of Al's class when you took it? I know when he was my teacher, he was absolutely brilliant."

"It was alright," I reply.

"Shay probably doesn't even remember most of it," Alan says. "It was a while ago."

Shelly looks back at me. "What did you end up getting your degree in?"

"Business," I reply. "I got my last couple of credits online."

"Oh, okay."

The funny thing is that she's not being rude. Even if I was obsessed with her man, she doesn't seem to be fazed by it in the slightest.

"So, how did you two meet?" I ask. "You were another student?"

She smiles. "I was a freshman and didn't know anyone. I was from a small town in Nebraska, and I was terrified. Al saw me listening to music one day and asked what it was. We talked, and he asked if I wanted to go for coffee."

You don't fucking say.

She giggles. "Who knew he was a secret Taylor Swift fan?"

"Mm-hmm," is all I can manage to get out.

Devon surprises me when he steps in and says, "I'm sorry, Alan, but isn't sleeping with your students considered a big no-no in the teaching world? Seems like it would go against some code of conduct or something."

Alan takes a sip of his drink before answering. "It's frowned upon, but there are no actual rules in place."

"Hm. Seems like there should be."

I let out a little laugh under my breath.

Shelly rubs her hands over his beard. "I knew from the first time I heard him speak that this was the man I was going to spend the rest of my life with."

Oh, gag me.

She goes on and on about their one-of-a-kind love story...that he somehow made work for whatever woman he was dating.

When he told me there was someone else that he really loved, I always sort of thought it would be somebody his own age. Maybe someone who was more suited to his lifestyle.

Turns out he picked someone who was even younger than me. According to Shelly, she started dating when she was only a freshman. I was a senior. I guess I must have seemed super old...in pervert years, that is.

I look her up and down and wonder what she had that I didn't. What about her made him fall so hard in love that he wanted to be with her over me?

Her red hair?

Her innocent demeanor?

The way she fawns all over him like she can't get enough?

Yeah, that's probably the one.

And he never told her what he did. He never told her that for an entire year of their relationship, he was fucking me.

He never had to answer for that.

He got to get off scot-free and get married and have babies while I got a whole assortment of issues that should probably keep me in therapy.

Why should he get to go around breaking hearts and then get to live happily ever after?

Did karma completely skip over him?

I zone back into the conversation just in time to hear Shelly saying, "I just can't get enough of him. That's why we already have four kids!"

The idea of that is enough to churn my stomach. I feel like I'm going to be sick as the weight of all of this hits me like a ton of bricks.

Turning to Devon, I try to keep my cool.

But it's no use, so I lean in really close so only he can hear me.

"Shark."

Chapter Twenty-six

DEVON

W e barely make it back to the room before Shay's in the bathroom throwing up her guts. I stand behind her, holding her hair back before grabbing her a rag that's wetted down with some cold water.

"It's alright. Just get it out," I say.

"I'm no better than Becky," she jokes once she's done.

"Becky was drunk. You've been gut punched. There's a difference," I tell her.

"Still, I ruined the night."

"You did no such thing." I reach over to the big bathtub and turn on the hot water.

There's a tiny bottle of bubble bath with the other toiletries that I open and add to the running water.

I reach for Shay's hand, and once I pull her to her feet, I start taking off her dress.

I've been thinking about doing this all night, but this isn't what I had in mind. I thought we would get through the dinner and come back here for a wild night, but right now, I don't think about any of that.

All I want to do is comfort her—to let her know that she's not alone in this. I'll be here for her in whatever way she needs me to be.

I watch every curve of her body come into view, but as much as I love the sight, I know me coming onto her right now isn't what she needs.

Before I move on to her bra, she walks over to the sink and quickly brushes her teeth.

"Sorry," she mutters. "Didn't want to have vomit breath."

"You don't need to apologize to me for shit."

Once her bra is off, the water in the tub is just about to the top, so I take her hand and help her in.

"Come in with me," she says.

"Why don't you just relax? I'll sit out here."

Her face drops a little before she murmurs, "Please."

Say no more.

I get out of all my clothes as fast as possible and get in the tub with her. She scoots forward, letting me climb in behind her before she leans back against my chest.

"Talk to me, beautiful," I whisper, running my fingers along her wet skin.

"I just had to get out of there." She pauses a moment, and I think maybe that's going to be the end of the conversation, but she keeps going. "You know, I've never really known what life would hold for me. I never really knew if I wanted to get married and have a family. I still don't know if I want that. But seeing Alan have it pisses me off. He shouldn't get to be happy after being such a dick."

I don't interrupt but just listen to her as she gets it all out.

"Once I finally got over the whole broken heart phase, it's not like I missed him. I realized how much of an asshole he was, and I realized I was better off. I just always thought he would eventually get what was coming to him. I don't think it's karma that he's living some bullshit perfect life."

"Maybe it's not perfect," I say.

"What do you mean?"

"I mean, maybe they just put on some huge act for everyone to try to give the illusion of happiness. Maybe she sits at home binge eating snack cakes in the closet, hiding from their kids while he won't turn off the football game."

She smiles. "I like that. And maybe their sex is super boring."

I laugh. "Oh, I know having anyone after having you must seem super boring. He downgraded for sure."

I know I'll probably feel that way once this week is over.

When we are both quiet for a moment, I say, "Shay. I'm so sorry."

"Why?"

"I feel like you having to deal with this is completely my fault. I asked you to come here with me just so I wouldn't have to be here alone." Guilt washes over me as I speak the words.

"Devon, you didn't twist my arm to come here. And I meant what I said when I told you I've had a really good time."

I still feel guilty but hearing her say she's had a good time helps a little. I hate that she had to deal with all this bullshit while here. First, Kyra, and then, Alan.

I never thought that someone would come along who would make Kyra seem not so bad, but I think Alan takes the cake. From the moment Shay told me he was her teacher, and he was perfectly okay with starting a relationship with his student, something didn't sit right with me. I get having an attraction to someone, but maybe wait until the semester is over?

When she told me how he kept stringing her along without promising any type of commitment, I knew exactly where the whole thing was heading. He took advantage of her being young and naïve.

And it seems that he did the same thing with Shelly. I wonder how many other times he'd run the same routine. A teacher getting into a relationship with a doting student. But this time, it was a far different outcome.

I'm guessing after he told Shay and got her reaction, he didn't want to risk Shelly walking out on him too. He decided to just ride the lie and hope for the best.

I guess for once, it worked out for him. I can only imagine how fast his world would come crashing down if Shelly knew the truth.

I ask, "Are you going to tell her?"

"Shelly?"

I nod.

She thinks for a moment. "I don't know. I really don't want to do anything that could ruin Becky and Dan's wedding. That isn't fair when this whole thing has absolutely nothing to do with them."

"You could wait until after the wedding. Tell her at the end of the night."

"Back then, I used to think about telling her. Of course, I had no idea who she was, but if I did, I think I would have. Now, I don't know. Part of me feels like it isn't my place. Then again, I don't know that the bastard deserves to be happy either."

I kiss her on the top of her head. "I wish I could make the decision for you, Sunshine."

"I know. We just have to get through tomorrow, and then, I can go home and forget this whole thing ever happened."

Her words hit me a little harder than expected. I know she's probably talking about Alan, but I wonder if she's also talking about everything that's happened between us.

But right now, it's not about me.

"How can I help, Shay? Tell me how I can help make this night a little bit better?"

She thinks for a moment. "I know I'm going to regret this, but I just need you to hold me. Hold me until I fall asleep."

If I didn't know how much Shay was hurting before, I sure as shit know now. Otherwise, there's no way she'd be asking me to cuddle.

But right now, I'd do anything she asked me to.

And honestly, I'm going to enjoy holding her all night long.

Chapter Twenty-seven

DEVON

The next morning, I leave Shay long enough to go do the actual wedding rehearsal—although I have no idea what we actually need to rehearse. It's walking down an aisle. How hard can that be?

I considered waking Shay up, but she was sleeping so hard. And I didn't want to wake her after the night she had last night.

While we are waiting to get this show on the road, Dan walks over to me. "Hey, man, everything okay? I got your text last night. Shelly's husband is Shay's ex-boyfriend?"

I nod. "Yeah, but try to keep that under your hat. I know she doesn't want it to get out. I just wanted to fill you in so that you would know why we left so early."

"Yeah, man. I get it. Do what you have to do. I hope you don't mind, but I told Becky."

I let out a long groan, but he says, "No, it's cool. She won't say anything. And she did you a solid. She actually moved Shelly and Alan to the other end of the table, so you guys can enjoy your night without having to interact with either of them."

"Wow," I say, almost unable to believe it. "I didn't think Becky would do that."

"Come on, Dev. She's not heartless. You know she cares about you. Plus, she felt like she owed Shay one after Shay took care of her the other night at the bar. I convinced her this would be the perfect opportunity to return the favor."

I chuckle. "I appreciate that."

"Did that put you in a good mood? Because now, I have to ruin it with some bad."

Another groan from me. "What now?"

"You're walking down the aisle with Kyra."

Motherfucker.

He goes on to say, "But I mean, it's not for very long. If you want, you can sprint down the aisle. Well, actually, don't do that. Becky will kill me. I guess if you do it, don't tell her it was my idea."

"It's fine," I interrupt him. "I can deal with Kyra for a couple minutes."

"If she starts acting up, I give Shay my full permission to kick her ass after we say *I do.*"

"She may just take you up on that offer."

Moments later, the wedding planner comes in and gets us all lined up. Kyra stands silently next to me, and I pray to God she stays that way. But of course, I'm not going to get that lucky.

With our arms linked together, we make our way down the aisle. Kyra says, "You know, I think Bruno really misses you. Maybe when this whole thing is over you can come see him sometime."

I don't even bother to look at her. "Quit fucking around, Kyra."

"I'm serious. I shouldn't have kept you from him the way that I did. To be honest, he probably likes you more than he does me."

Because the dog can probably tell how awful you are.

She goes on to add, "Maybe we could go grab a cup of coffee or something."

To most, this act Kyra is putting on might be somewhat believable. But not to me. I know she's full of shit. This is all some sort of ploy. She's hoping she can worm her way back into my life so that she can somehow stick it to Shay. Kyra isn't happy unless everyone around her is as miserable as she is.

"Not going to happen," I tell her.

"Why not? Don't you miss me?" She playfully asks.

Not wanting to deal with her shit, I reply with, "You know what? I really don't."

She goes to say something else, but we reach the end of the aisle and part ways.

Thank God.

I don't care if Shay is my just *pretend* girlfriend. I'm not about to go running back to my ex who treated me like something she stepped in.

No way in hell.

When the rehearsal is over, I get a text on my phone. I pull it out, hoping it's from Shay, but instead it's a text from Duke.

Duke: How's it going with the fake girlfriend? Is everyone buying it?

Me: Damn dude, the week is almost over now. You're a little late to the party, but yeah, I think everyone's buying it. We've hit some trouble, though.

Duke: How so?

Me: Kyra has been an ass all week. I'm surprised Shay hasn't beat her up yet. And last night, a guy showed up who happens to be Shay's ex-boyfriend.

Seconds after I hit send, my phone starts ringing.

"Hello?" I say, walking away from everyone else.

Duke says, "Hi—"

Avery interrupts him, clearly on speakerphone. "Tell us everything!"

"Really?" I ask. "You're in on this too?"

"Yes!" She squeals. "And I'm invested. This is the most exciting thing that has happened lately."

Duke says, "I feel like I should be offended."

Avery says, "Oh, you know I love you. But hush. Let your brother speak."

"You two sound like you're watching a soap opera," I tell them. "But look, I'm surrounded by a ton of people right now. How about after I get back, I take you two out for a beer, and I'll tell you all about it."

Avery sighs. "Fine. But it better be soon. We know where you live, Samson!"

We hang up the phone, and I decide to take a little walk before heading back to the room. I don't want to wake Shay up until I absolutely have to.

I hate that this is our last day together. I'm not ready to give her up.

Maybe that's because I'm falling for her.

Hard.

I never fathomed that the spunky goth bartender from my local watering hole would be someone that I have such strong feelings for. But here we are.

I'm well aware of how ridiculous the whole thing sounds. We pretend to be boyfriend and girlfriend for a week, and now, I'm falling in love with her? Sounds insane. But it's true.

I'd like to keep this thing going—to do it for real and see where it goes. But I'm not sure if Shay wants that. She seems to be very anti-relationship. I'm not sure that a few days of us being together is going to change that. And I certainly don't want to push her into something she's not ready for.

As I'm walking outside, my thoughts are interrupted when someone goes to pass me but accidentally bumps my shoulder.

"Oh, I'm sorry," the man says.

I look over and see that it's Alan.

"It's fine," I say with a small nod. I start to walk away, but he stops me.

"You're dating Shay, right?"

I'm sure he already knows the answer to that, but I say yes anyway.

"She's a good girl," he says. "You're a lucky man."

"I know," I tell him. "She's the best. But I guess you already know that, don't you?"

He rubs his hand over his beard. "I see Shay has told you about me."

"Yeah, you came up," I reply, shoving my hands in my pockets. Maybe if they're secured, they won't haul off and hit him.

"Look," he begins. "I never meant to hurt her."

"You strung along a young, naïve girl who was head-over-heels in love with you. You promised her the world on a silver platter, and then, you told her that there was someone else. I honestly don't believe that you thought she'd come out of this whole thing unscathed. And to top it all off, she has to come here and find out the girl you cheated on her with knows nothing of your infidelity. And you gave her all the things you promised to Shay."

"I didn't know Shay would be here."

"Well, obviously," I say. "But you just don't get it, do you? You could have run into her at the supermarket, and it would have been the same result. This wedding has nothing to do with it. Let's just call this what it is—a predatory teacher who had a thing for students who he could manipulate. I may be wrong, but I think they call that grooming."

"I did love her," he defends.

"Bullshit. You don't do that to someone you love. You loved the idea of her. You loved that she was young and cute, and you loved that she stroked your ego. But now, I hope that you look back and understand exactly what you gave up."

I start to walk away, but I guess Alan has one final question. "Do you think she will tell?"

"What?" I ask, looking back at him.

"Do you think Shay will tell Shelly?"

This guy.

"I don't know. I know she doesn't want to ruin Dan and Becky's day."

He lets out a clear sigh of relief. Not wanting him to feel like he's off the hook, I add, "But I can't say you'll get that lucky with me. The moment the two of them say their vows, I make no promises that I'll keep my mouth shut. Assholes shouldn't get happily ever after's."

I walk away before he can say another word.

I hope the bastard is scared for the rest of the day.

Chapter Twenty-eight

SHAY

M y eyes slowly open, taking in the room around me. Despite me staying here all week, it takes me a moment to realize where I am. When it clicks, everything from the past twenty-four hours comes rushing back.

Reaching behind me, I feel for Devon. Of course, my first thought is that if he's there, I can climb on top of him and try to forget everything.

But all I find is a piece of paper with a note scribbled on it.

Had to go to the wedding rehearsal. Be back soon.
Xoxo
Dev

Or maybe I won't be able to occupy my mind with something else.

I roll over onto my back, rubbing my eyes as I try to process the events of yesterday.

I always feared the day I would run into Alan. We only live a couple of small towns apart, so I knew it would happen eventually. What are the chances I run into him at a wedding that's not even close to where we live?

I've wondered what I would do when I saw him. Would I yell? Would I cry? Would I run the other direction, trying to avoid him?

Much to my surprise, I didn't do any of those things.

And luckily for me, I didn't run into him somewhere that I was alone. I had Devon.

Last night, I figured the universe must hate me for bringing Alan back into my life at this wedding of all places, but now, I think I should count my lucky stars that it was here. Devon was here with me and got me through it. I had him to lean on when I was mid panic-attack, and he was here to take my mind off of it when I asked him to.

Maybe this was when it was supposed to happen.

I'm not sure if I even believe in any of that kind of stuff, but the thought of it now is oddly comforting.

And now that I've had a good night's sleep, the whole thing really doesn't feel like that big of a deal.

Is Alan an asshole?

Yes.

Did seeing him bring up a lot of memories that I've tried to shove down deep inside for many years?

Also, yes.

But I survived. And now, I'm fine. The worst is over, and I can get back to shoving all my feelings back down where they belong.

Maybe it's not the healthiest option, but it's worked out for me so far.

A few minutes later, Devon creeps back into the room, trying to be quiet in case I'm still asleep.

"I'm awake, Cassanova," I tell him.

"Oh, good. I suck at being quiet." He laughs.

"Well, I didn't wake up when you left, so I guess you're better than you think."

He walks over and takes a seat on the edge of the bed. "How are you doing?"

"I'm okay," I tell him.

He smiles. "Of course, you are."

"I know I always say I'm okay, but I promise it's true. You took good care of me, and I'm feeling much better this morning."

"Good."

"Thank you for being here last night."

He rubs his fingertips over my arm. "Anything for you."

He looks over at the clock. "We should probably start getting ready. Are you ready to pretend to be my girlfriend one more time?"

Grabbing his hand, I smile. "Let's go to a wedding."

After the vows have been read, dinner has been served, and the cake has been cut, everything seems to be winding down for the evening. Some people have even started to leave already, but Devon and I choose to join a few other couples in dancing for a bit. We've been so busy trying to make the most of our last couple hours of pretending to be a couple that I have barely even noticed Alan—or Kyra for that matter.

"So, do you think everyone bought it?" I ask Devon as he twirls me around the dance floor. "Do people believe we are a couple?"

"Well, no one here is staring at us the way they were the first night we did this, so I'd say there's a pretty good chance."

Devon gives me a light kiss. "But just to be sure." He smiles.

Kissing him makes me realize how much I'm going to miss those soft lips of his. The man certainly knows how to kiss—among other things. I'm going to miss that tongue of his too. I consider suggesting that we keep doing a friends-with-benefits thing when we get back home, but I could see how that could get really messy.

It would probably be better if I set Mr. Pussy free to go please someone else for a while. After all, one shouldn't keep the elusive white whale in captivity so to speak.

As if able to tell that I'm thinking dirty thoughts about him, Devon follows suit. "You know, when I see you now, it's not going to be the same knowing that you're wearing underwear again. I kind of liked knowing that you were going without them."

I look up at him and smile. "Who said I always wear underwear?"

He closes his eyes and sighs. "Great. Now, every time I see you, I'm going to wonder whether or not you are."

"You're welcome," I tease.

"What did you think of the wedding?" He asks.

"Eh, it was a wedding." I shrug. "I liked that it was short, sweet, and to the point."

"Me too. The whole week was so drawn out, maybe they decided to keep that part to the bare minimum."

"You looked handsome walking down the aisle," I tell him. "Even though you had to do it with Kyra."

"Well, thanks." He grins.

"Did she say anything bitchy to you?"

"No, she didn't say a word. I think she's still mad at me for yesterday."

"What happened yesterday?" I ask, feeling like I'm missing something.

"Oh, I forgot to tell you. During the rehearsal, she told me that I should come over and see the dog, and maybe she and I could go get coffee."

"And what did you say?" I don't know why my gut clenches as I wait for the answer. After today, why do I give a fuck what he does with his time?

"I told her I'm with you, and as much as I miss the dog, I'm not going over there to see her, have coffee, or anything else."

"What about when this whole thing is over? Do you think you'll ever get back together with her?"

"Hell no." He replies without hesitation.

Despite Devon being my fake boyfriend, knowing he isn't going back to her gives me a sense of smug pride.

We dance in silence for a minute, just trying to enjoy our remaining time together when he says, "I know this will probably sound lame to you, but I'm going to miss you when this whole thing is said and done."

"Doesn't sound lame," I tell him.

"I was thinking maybe when we get back..."

As he talks, I can already see where this is going, but I'm not ready for that. I'm not ready to make any promises that I know I can't keep. And when we get back, I just want my life to go back to the way that it was. I'll miss Devon like crazy, and maybe a little part of me could see him being someone that I could actually be with.

But I don't think I'm ready to be with anyone. I don't want to get my heart broken again, and with how I feel about Devon, I know that he has the ability to shatter it.

I don't want to take that chance.

"Hold that thought," I tell him, hoping that I can find a way to avoid the subject altogether. "I'm going to go hit up the bar. You want anything?"

"Uh, no, I'm good. Do you want me to get it for you?"

"I've got it," I say, already starting to walk away. "Be right back."

When I get to the bar, it's the same bartender that's been working the entire time we've been here. Before I can open my mouth, he hands me some tequila.

"Bless you," I say.

I'm pretty sure he likes me because one night while he was working, I shoved a hundred-dollar bill in his tip jar. Being a bartender, I know how important tips are. I'm damn sure going to pay it forward.

I take a sip, letting the strong tequila coat my throat on the way down. I tell myself I'm going to nurse this one and let it be my only one of the evening.

But a familiar voice next to me tells me that I'm going to need another.

"Hello, Shay."

"Alan," I reply while looking into my glass instead of at him.

"Can we go somewhere and talk?"

I'm tempted to tell him to go fuck himself. I tell myself that there's not a thing in the world that I want to say to him right now.

But that would be a lie.

For years, I've thought about what I would say to him if we ever got the chance to actually talk. Even though I've gone out of my way to avoid any type of conversation, I still think maybe some type of closure would be nice.

"Fine," I spit. I point at the bartender. "I'll be back, my friend. Keep 'em coming."

He nods and smiles, and I follow Alan out into one of the hallways. He then takes a turn into what looks like a small banquet room. There are some tables set up with fancy tablecloths on them and decorative center pieces in the middle. I wonder if this is where they would have moved the reception if it had rained.

"Shall we sit?" He asks, gesturing to one of the tables.

"No. I don't intend on this taking long," I say, but he sits anyway.

"Alright," he says, sounding a little surprised by my answer. "I didn't know you'd be here."

"Okay? Is that supposed to make me feel better about this whole thing? Or you for that matter?"

"I don—"

"What if you had known I was coming? Would it have mattered? No. You still would have showed up. The only difference is you probably would have reached out beforehand so that we could get our stories straight. Speaking of which, how dare you. How dare you pretend that what we had was nothing."

"Shay, it wasn't nothing. But you were just so young."

222

I point my finger at him. "Don't start that shit with me, Alan. I've met your wife, remember? She's younger than me!"

He plays with a strand of his beard between his thumb and forefinger. "I'm not sure what you want me to say."

"Oh, you don't know? Allow me to enlighten you. I want you to tell me why. I want you to tell me why you lied to me for over a year. I want you to tell me why you told me the truth, but you didn't tell Shelly. And I want to know why you didn't pick me. As it stands, I'm happy you didn't pick me. Things worked out for the better, but I want to know why."

He takes another sip of his drink before he starts talking. "I started dating you and Shelly about the same time. I had two gorgeous students interested in me, and I didn't know who to pick. I liked you both, so I decided to start seeing the two of you casually and see where it went. I didn't fathom I'd end up falling in love with both of you."

I can't help but roll my eyes. "You should have ended it with one of us long before you did. It wasn't right stringing us along."

"You're right. I just couldn't figure out how to say goodbye to one of you."

"And you liked getting your dick wet twice. I bet it gave you some sort of crazy satisfaction sleeping with two girls who were polar opposites."

"Man, I forgot how blunt you are."

"Yeah," I say. "I've gotten worse. I'm no longer that young naïve girl who follows you around like a lost puppy. What you did pretty much knocked that right out of me."

He looks down at his hands, fiddling with his wedding ring.

Really?

Do we think now's the best time to be messing with your wedding ring?

Since he's just sitting there like a lump, I decide to continue. "I need to know why. Why her? What did she have that I didn't?"

"Why does it matter? Can't we just say that you and I weren't meant to be and leave it at that?"

Narrowing my eyes at him, I ask, "What the fuck do you think?"

The more I talk, the more I realize that it's any sadness I once had over this man has been replaced with something else.

Rage.

Going on, I say, "You told me back then that you came clean to her. You told me that there were no secrets, but come to find out, you didn't tell her any of it. I deserve to know why."

"I was in love with her. She was the one. I couldn't risk losing her the way I lost you."

"Be honest, Alan. You knew you'd lose me. You knew I wasn't the type of girl to stick around while you *figured things out.* Deep down, you had to know I'd never go for that."

"You're right. I knew me coming clean would mean you leaving me."

"And that made it easier for you. You didn't have to be the bad guy and break up with me. You tried leaving the decision in my hands."

He nods. "I suppose."

"I want to know why her. What made her *the one?*"

"Honestly?" He waits for me to say yes before saying, "Because she needs me."

"Come again?"

"Shay, when you and I were together, you didn't need me. You were independent as hell. You had this big, beautiful brain that I adored, but I didn't want someone who was going to give me a run for my money. I was already in my mid-thirties. I was looking for someone to settle down with. Someone who wanted to get married and have babies."

I interrupt him. "You and I talked about that stuff. You knew I wasn't against that."

"But I also knew you had dreams. You wanted to try to take on the world first. And I didn't want to stand in your way."

Classic Alan. Trying to turn a situation where he's the villain into one where he's a martyr.

Piss off.

"So, you wanted a doormat?"

"I wanted a wife. A good wife. I wanted someone to be waiting for me when I got home from work with dinner on the table and a smile on her face. Let's be honest, Shay. That was never going to be you."

Oh, so he wanted a 1950's wife.

225

I never thought being labeled as independent would be a bad thing. But I guess some men would rather have a *yes* woman than one who speaks her mind.

He's right. I'll never be that girl.

I'd rather stay single for the rest of my life than turn into someone without a voice or opinion.

He goes on to say, "You never needed me. Shelly does. She treats me like I'm the most important thing in her life."

I don't understand how those two things are mutually exclusive. Someone can be the most important person in my life without me needing to rely on them for everything.

In barely more than a whisper, I say, "You should have never made me love you. I've never hidden who I am—even back then. You knew what you were getting into."

"And you were fun, Shay. But fun only goes so far."

Those words punch me in the gut. Alan never told me any of this back in the day. He just told me that he had been seeing someone else and that he was in love with her too. He was conflicted or some bullshit. He never told me why.

Now that I know, I realize just how much of an asshole he really is.

How did I really love him?

I've spent years wondering what it was that truly happened. Turns out he's just a jerk.

"Thank you for this," I tell him. "You've given me closure on something that I never knew if I would have."

"I'm sorry you got hurt in the whole thing," he says.

"Save it. I just don't care anymore." I start to walk away, but he stops me.

"That man of yours is really crazy about you."

I stop walking. "What makes you say that?"

"This morning, he gave me an earful about how amazing you are and how stupid I was to let you go. He seems to really love you."

If that were true, it would give me a sense of smugness. I could leave here and go home to the guy who loves me and live happily ever after.

But that's not the case. I'm going home to be alone. Although I like it that way, it doesn't make this situation any easier.

Starting to walk again, I say, "Goodbye, Alan."

"Are you going to tell Shelly? About you and me back then?"

I think for a moment before giving my answer.

Leaving Alan in my past, I say, "Didn't you hear me? I don't care anymore."

As I head back to Devon, my head spins. Eight years is a hell of a long time to hold onto something. I'm not sure if knowing the truth makes me feel better or worse.

The only thing I'm sure about is that I'm exhausted.

And I think it's about time this eventful week come to an end.

Chapter Twenty-nine

SHAY

"**I**'m sorry I wanted to leave," I tell Devon on our way home. We've already been driving for a couple of hours, and it's been pretty quiet. I can't tell if Dev is pissed at me or not.

"It's alright," he says. "We stayed for the important stuff."

"I just couldn't be there anymore."

He looks over at me. "Do you want to tell me what happened?"

"What do you mean?"

"I saw you go talk to Alan. Then, you come back ready to get the hell out of dodge. What did you two talk about that got you so frazzled?"

I consider not telling him, but he's been so great this week, and I don't want to start being bitchy now.

"I pretty much asked him why he did what he did."

"And did he give a reason?"

I sigh. "He gave a lot of reasons. None of them good or worthy of the shit he pulled. But that's Alan—always trying to justify why he does things instead of just owning up to them."

"This is probably going to sound bad, but I'm so glad you didn't marry that guy."

"Me too."

"What else did he say?"

I start fiddling with my fingernails. "I asked him why Shelly. Why did he choose to tell me yet keep her in the dark so that he could be with her."

Devon doesn't speak but just waits for me to continue.

"He told me that I was too independent. He wanted someone who would *need* him. He wanted a woman who didn't push or give him a run for his money. His words, not mine."

Devon's face contorts. "Are you fucking kidding me?"

"What?" I ask, confused as to why he's so heated.

"He thinks you being independent is a bad thing? That's the most ridiculous bullshit I've ever heard. That's something that's awesome."

"You wouldn't want a girl who has to depend on you for everything?"

"Fuck no!" He pauses for a second. "Look, do I understand that sometimes, it may feel nice to feel needed. Sure, I get that. But you know what feels better? To be *wanted*. Shay, whoever gets the privilege of being with you for the rest of their life will be lucky as hell because you will be with them

229

because you want to. Not because you need to. If I wanted someone who needed me, I'd get a puppy."

That manages to get a smile out of me.

He continues, "You have your own life, your own money, your own interests—all of that is a good thing. It means that you're not likely to change for someone else. If he can't see the value of that, then, fuck him."

"I guess he just wanted someone who was going to tell him yes all the time. He wanted to mold someone into his perfect version of a wife. That's not me. According to him, I'm too much of a handful."

Reaching over to me, he takes my hand in his. "Shay, anyone who thinks you're a handful just doesn't have big enough hands."

"He told me what you said to him."

"He did?" He looks nervous like I'm going to be mad.

"Thank you for standing up for me."

"You're welcome, but all I did was speak the truth. You're awesome, and he's an idiot for giving you up."

Yet again, Devon knows just what to say to make me feel better. Vulnerability isn't something that I often show to people. If the events of this week hadn't played out the way they had, I doubt I would have shown any weakness at all to Devon. That's just not who I am. I'm stoic to a fault.

Even around those I love—or hell, even when I'm alone—I rarely let out my emotions. It's easier to just act like I'm fine, and eventually, I am.

This week, I've had Devon around to help me deal with everything. He's hyped me up, made me laugh, or just listened. It may have only been a few days, but I've gotten kind of used to it.

And now, I won't have it anymore. An overwhelming sadness hits me at that fact. Sure, we can still be friends, I'm sure I'll see him at the bar. But how awkward is that going to be? How am I going to feel about it when I see him trying to pick up other women to take home?

It shouldn't bother me at all. He's not my boyfriend. We fucked for a week.

That's it.

As much as I keep telling myself that, it feels like it was more than just that.

But I don't do relationships, and neither does Devon. He's still got a lot of women to ruin for other men, and I just don't feel like dealing with men's shit in general.

This whole week, we've held onto the notion that this whole thing is temporary. I'm sure I'm just all up in my feelings now because it's ending.

But once again, I push those feelings down and tell myself I'm fine.

The rest of the ride home goes quickly. We move on from talking about Alan to just the wedding in general and then make some other random small talk.

Soon enough, he's pulling his truck into my drive.

"Hm," I say, looking at the cars in the driveway.

"What?"

"That's my dad's car, but I don't see Suzie's."

Quickly, he helps me with my bags, setting them on the porch.

With his hands in his pockets, he says, "Thanks for coming with me. You were amazing all week."

"Thanks for inviting me. I had fun."

There's a slight moment of awkwardness between us, but then, he leans in, gently grabbing my face. "One more time for the road."

He kisses me.

This time, the kiss is filled with all the things we want to say to each other but keep to ourselves instead. It's filled with a week's worth of fun and memories.

It's perfect.

When he pulls back, a sudden wave of emotion hits me, but I do my best to keep it contained.

As he walks away, he asks, "When do you want me to come finish the cabinets?"

"Uhhh, I don't know. I'll call you."

"Sounds good, Sunshine. Talk to you soon."

I don't watch him drive away but instead head right inside. Bones is at the door, his nubby little tail wagging 90 miles a minute.

"Hey, boy," I say, showering him with love.

Dad and Pops walk out from the kitchen.

Dad smiles, "Sweetheart, you're home!"

"Is Suzie okay?" I ask.

"Oh, she's fine. Her mom took a fall, so she called to see if we could come hang out with Bones until you got home."

"Oh, okay. Good. Glad you guys are here."

Looking me up and down, he asks, "Sweetheart, are you okay?"

The moment he says the words, the dam of emotion I've been holding in suddenly breaks. In the blink of an eye, I'm practically sobbing as I answer, "No."

He rushes over to me, wrapping me in a hug. Looking at Pops, he says, "Honey, can you go to the store? We're going to need ice cream. And wine. Lots of wine."

Chapter Thirty

DEVON

*T*wo *weeks later.*

"How was Hawaii?" I ask Becky and Dan who sit across from me.

"Wonderful!" Becky practically sings.

They got home yesterday, and I asked if I could come talk to them today. Becky took it as the perfect opportunity to break out some of her new wedding gifts and have a snack board and mimosas out on their deck.

Ever since we got back from the wedding, I've been miserable. I never fathomed I'd miss my fake girlfriend as much as I do. I've been trying to get ahold of her to talk...or just to finish her kitchen, but she hasn't returned any of my calls. And the only texts she's sent have just been telling me that she's been busy. She even dropped my tools off outside my house so that I wouldn't have to come get them.

I had this grand idea in my head that I was going to tell her how I felt about her. I was going to try to convince her to give this thing a shot, but the way she's acting shows me that she doesn't want that. I guess this whole thing meant more to me than it did to her.

Or maybe dealing with Kyra all week and then seeing Alan was just too much for her. My favor forced her to deal with something that she's been avoiding for years. I can't imagine that was easy.

And I could kick the bastard's ass for telling her all those things that he didn't like about her. How dare he make her feel like she was less than worthy because she actually has a brain.

Fuck that guy.

He better hope I never run into him again.

Dan pulls me from my thoughts. "So, you wanted to talk. What's up?"

Becky adds, "Where's Shay?"

"That's what I needed to talk to you about."

"Oh?" She asks, downing half her mimosa.

"Look, I lied to you guys. Shay's not my girlfriend. Never was. She just did me a favor by coming to the wedding so that I could win the bet."

They both sit in silence, and I wonder what they're thinking. I brace myself for the inevitable earful I'm about to get from Becky.

Dan is the first to speak, though. He asks, "So, you two weren't banging? I could swear that you two were—"

Becky cuts him off. "Of course, they were banging. They just weren't in a relationship. Isn't that right, Devon?"

I nod.

Here it comes.

To lessen the blow, I pull an envelope from my pocket and slide it across the table. "Here. It's the money that I owe you or your parents or whoever."

Becky's eyes flick down to look at it, but she doesn't grab it. "Why? Why tell us now? Why not just make up some sort of excuse as to why the two of you broke up? We never would have known the difference."

"Because Shay has had enough lies told about her by a man. I don't want to follow suit. I don't want to be someone just making up another lie about her."

She stares at me intently, making me feel like I'm about to be interrogated about something.

"You have feelings for her, don't you?"

I was right.

I guess I shouldn't start lying now.

"Yeah, Beck, I do. But it doesn't really matter. I don't think she feels the same way about me, so we are both just moving on with our lives."

"You're both idiots. Fucking idiots."

"Come again?" I ask.

"Look, I can tell when someone's faking feelings. You two may have put on a good show, but neither of you are *that* good. It was obvious there was a connection between the two of you."

"I hate to break it to you, Becky, but I think it was just me that had the feelings."

"Have you told her about your feelings?" She asks.

"When I call, she doesn't answer. When I text, she just blows me off. So, I'm guessing she doesn't want things to go any further."

She takes a bite of one of the crackers on her snack tray. "I think you should go tell her how you feel."

"Did you not just hear me? She doesn't want to see me." I say each word slowly, hoping she will comprehend it more this time.

"Make her listen."

"Have you met Shay?" I retort. "She's not doing a damn thing she doesn't want to."

I go on to say, "Look, I'm sorry I lied. I pushed off the whole idea of finding a girlfriend until the last second, and then, I begged Shay to be my date. I shouldn't have done that."

Becky smiles. "As far as dates go, Shay wasn't a bad one. I liked having her around."

"Me too," I say in barely more than a whisper.

"Do you miss her?" Dan asks.

"Yeah, all the fucking time. I haven't even attempted to bring anyone home with me since I've been back. Just doesn't even seem like a good time anymore."

Dan sighs. "Shit man, I'm sorry."

"I'll get over it. Eventually, my dick will win out, and I'm sure I'll find someone to take my mind off Shay. Until then, I'll just go to work, come home and sleep before doing it all over again."

Becky slides the envelope back over to me. "Here, you keep this."

"But I cheated. Pretty sure that means I lost the bet."

She shrugs her shoulders. "Fuck the bet. You brought someone who ended up making our wedding week a little better. You don't owe me anything after that. Besides, all I ask is that you go get her. Do your best to win her over because honestly, we may pick her over you if we have to choose."

I know she's joking, but I can't say I'd blame her. Shay's awesome.

"I don't know how," I tell her.

"Devon, you are charming to a fault. You never have a problem getting women to go home with you. Use some of that charm to get Shay to give this thing a chance."

I have no idea how I'm going to do it, but I owe it to both of us to give it a try.

Chapter Thirty-one

SHAY

I head to the back room of the bar to grab a couple new bottles of Jack Daniels. The afternoon has been slow, so I've been trying to do as much upkeep around the bar as I can.

Anything to keep me busy and out of my own head.

The past couple weeks have sucked. Ever since we got back from the wedding, Devon has been trying to pinpoint a time to come over and finish my cabinets, but I've avoided him at every turn.

I don't know that I can see him and keep my hands to myself.

Or keep from bursting into tears.

That seems to be my new normal lately. Every time I think about him, I start to cry.

I never cry.

About anything.

Yet here I am, crying over a guy I was playing house with for a few days.

I'm not even really sure why I'm crying so much. Sure, I miss him, but that can't be the only reason. Maybe now I just associate him with all the emotional trauma that happened from running into Alan.

No, I know that isn't true either because I haven't thought about Alan at all.

Only Devon.

I've considered calling and telling him how I feel, but I stop myself every time. He's only calling me because he owes me the favor of fixing my kitchen. Since I'm so hard-headed, I'm sure he's already moved on to spending time between another woman's legs now. I doubt that he goes very long without getting laid.

Me, on the other hand? Well, I have a drawer full of vibrators to keep me company. I don't need any men in my life right now.

Especially because I'm sure they'll all be a letdown after Devon.

Just the thought of what his tongue can do gets me all tingly.

How's anyone supposed to compare to that?

So, instead of searching for someone who may live up to that high standard, I'll just do it myself...with the help of my battery-powered friends.

I just dread the day when Devon brings one of his new lady friends into the bar, or worse, I have to see him attempting to pick up women in here. He hasn't been in here since we got back. Part of me wants to see him walk through the door, but part of me wants him to stay far away.

Suzie pokes her head into the back room. "Hey, there's someone here to see you."

No fucking way.

Before I can ask who it is, she's already disappeared from the doorway. I follow her to the front, filled with a combination of excitement and fear.

But when I see who it is, all I feel is confusion.

"Becky?" I ask.

"Hey, Shay." She looks over the specialty cocktail menu in front of her. "Can I get a blue hurricane?"

"Uh, sure," I stammer, immediately getting to work on making it.

When I finish, I slide it in front of her, and she takes a sip.

"Oh, that's good."

"Becky, not trying to be rude. I love that you're here buying booze, but I'm sure there's another reason you're here."

She stirs her drink with the straw. "Devon came to see us the other day. Told us that your little show was all an act."

"Oh," I say, not quite sure how else to respond. "I'm sorry. I didn't mean to like make a mockery out of your wedding or anything."

She holds her hand up to stop me. "It's alright. I'm not mad."

"Why'd he tell you?" I ask. "I thought we did a pretty good job of acting it out."

"You did. We were totally snowed. But he told me that enough lies have been told about you by men. He didn't want to be one of them by making up an excuse as to why you two broke up."

An unexpected smile touches my lips. "That sounds like something he'd say. What did you say when he came clean about everything?" I start wiping down the bar to give me something to do.

"I told him I thought you were both being idiots."

That gets me to stop and look at her again. "Why?"

"Because you can only fake that stuff so much, Shay. Acting will only get you so far. I came here to tell you the same thing I told him. Stop being stupid. You two should just go for it."

"It's not that easy," I tell her.

"Why? Because of what happened with Alan?"

"Do you know everything?" I ask in shock.

"Not quite. But Devon did give Dan the short version, and of course, Dan told me. I'm going to tell you something that I've never told anyone—well except for Dan."

She takes a deep breath before continuing. "Before Dan and I got together, I was with an awful son of a bitch. He was a drunk—an angry one. It started out with him just yelling. Then, it turned into him punching holes in the walls. Then...well, let's just say it turned into more. I called the cops, and the asshole went to jail. But I never thought I would trust another man again. When Dan came along, I was so nervous. It took him forever to even get me to agree to go out with him, but once I did, it didn't take long to realize that not all men are the same. Not all men are assholes."

When she takes a break, I ask, "Why are you telling me this?"

"Because I think you already know that Devon's not like the rest. Sure, he likes to go out and have fun with a slew of women, but only when he's single. When he's with a woman, he's beyond loyal. Even with as awful as Kyra treated him at times, he still stayed and loved her so hard. And I meant what I said that night in the bathroom. I've never seen him look at anyone the way he looks at you."

"I'm surprised you remember that night."

She laughs. "Me too. I just don't want you to give up on Devon just because Alan hurt you. Don't take Alan's mistakes out on Devon. He doesn't deserve that."

"Even if I did take your advice, I'm sure it's too late. He's probably already in bed with someone new."

"I can assure you he's not."

"How do you know?"

She rolls her eyes. "Because ever since we got back from our honeymoon, he's wanted to spend every spare minute he's not working with my husband in an attempt to keep his mind off of you. He hasn't been with anyone or gone out on the prowl. He sits on my couch like a lump most evenings doing nothing but talking about you. I need you to come get him." I think she's only half-joking.

"Why hasn't he said anything to me?"

"He said he's been trying to call and text, but you keep blowing him off."

"It's just been hard to talk to him," I say in a low voice.

"I know. But as I said, you're both being idiots. Get over your bullshit and call each other. Do whatever you need to do because clearly, you both are in a funk and need the other one to get out of it."

While she finishes her drink, I ask her all about Hawaii, which gets her talking about herself for a while. I only half pay attention because I'm still processing everything she said. If everything she told me is true, then, I guess Devon is feeling the same way I am.

Maybe we *are* both being idiots.

When she said he hadn't seen anyone else and couldn't stop talking about me, a certain happiness washed over me. That has to mean something, right?

When Becky finally leaves, I pull out my phone, trying to decide what I want to text Devon. Do I say what I need to say over a text? Should I call?

No, this is probably something we should discuss in person.

How can I get him over to my place without being too obvious?

Finally, I start typing.

Me: Hey, if you've got some free time tonight or tomorrow, would you want to come over and work on the kitchen? If not, no big deal. I know it's short notice.

It takes less than a minute for a reply to come through.

Devon: Sure. Tonight works. See you about seven.

There's my smile again. Now, I just have to figure out what the fuck I'm going to say.

Chapter Thirty-two

DEVON

T his is it.

This is my opportunity to tell Shay how I really feel about her.

When she texted me asking me to come over and work on her kitchen, I jumped at the chance. I still plan on honoring my end of the deal, but I'll be damned if I don't come clean about how much I miss her.

As I pull into her driveway, my heart feels like it is about to beat out of my chest.

Before I get very far, Shay walks out onto the porch with Bones who plops down right next to her.

"Hey," she greets.

Damn, she looks good. She's wearing a pair of ripped jeans and a black tank top instead of a t-shirt. She's got her piercings back in and her usual dark makeup.

Still fucking gorgeous.

No matter what, she's gorgeous.

"Hi," I say.

"Come inside—"

Before my brain can get ahead of it, my mouth starts moving. "Actually, I need to say something first."

It's now or never. I feel like if I follow her in there and get to work, I'm going to lose all my nerve. We will end up just making small talk, and I'll leave with all of this still weighing heavily on me. I can't do that.

"I love you," I blurt. That's not how I wanted to start this whole thing.

But I keep going because there's no turning back now.

"I know that sounds insane. We hung out for the better part of a week, and I'm telling you I love you. Sounds like a damn princess movie or something. And a few weeks ago, I would have said there was no way in hell. But then, I got to know you. And how amazing you are. You're by far, the most unique person I've ever met. You are so unapologetically *you*. And I fell hard."

"Dev," she begins.

I'm still not done, though. "Just let me finish. Please. You can kick me out when I'm done. If you tell me we're finished, I will leave you alone. But fuck, I hope you don't say that because these past couple weeks without you have sucked. All I can do is think about you. Dan told me that he knew Becky was the one because he realized his life was better

247

with her in it than without her. I'm here to tell you that my life has been awful without you, Sunshine. The first night we were together, I told everyone that I didn't realize what was right in front of me. Turns out it was true."

I walk toward her, meeting her on the porch. "I know that Alan hurt you. I know that because of him, you are scared to get hurt again, but Shay, I promise I won't hurt you. I'm not asking you for forever. I'm just asking if maybe you will consider giving this thing a shot. You and me. We can just see where it goes. And if it doesn't work, I promise that it won't be because I did something that hurt you."

She stands there silently, and I'm worried I've scared her off. She's probably going to tell me to fuck off or that this is all too much for her. Then, I'm not quite sure what I'll do. I haven't considered what may happen beyond this point.

"Shay, say something."

"You told me to let you finish." She crosses her arms over her chest. "Are you done?"

Oh boy, she's mad.

"Yeah, I'm done."

"Come inside," she says heading in through the front door.

Oh yeah, definitely mad.

I follow her inside and stop, taking in the room around me.

The room is dark except for the twenty candles that she has lit and scattered on every surface.

"What's going on?" I ask.

"Well, I called you here to tell you some things of my own, but you wanted to go first."

"Okay, I'm listening."

She stands in front of me, looking up at me with her pretty eyes. "I've missed you too."

She could end it there, and I'd be happy, but she keeps going. "I haven't ever even thought about being with anyone seriously since Alan. You and I pretended we were serious for a stupid bet, and somehow, it all just felt right. I'm not saying I'm going to be any good at this. And I'll probably drive you crazy, but if you are willing to try, so am I."

"Really?"

She shrugs her shoulders. "Yes, Cassanova. Because maybe I love you too."

I grab her and pull her close, crashing my lips against hers. Fuck, I've missed this.

When I look back at her, I say, "You just made me the happiest man in the whole fucking world."

"You're not going to miss all the other pussy you were getting?"

"You mean I have to give that up?" I tease, causing her to punch me in the shoulder.

"Devon," she warns.

"Okay, okay, I'm sorry. No, I'm not going to miss it. You are all that I need."

I pull her in to kiss her again, this time, grabbing her shirt to pull over her head.

I'll prove to her that she's the only one I want or need.

And I'll prove it to her every day for the rest of our lives.

Epilogue

SHAY

"**I**s this really all the clothes that you have?" I ask Devon as I situate them in my closet.

Well, I guess it's *our* closet now since he's moving in with me.

He eyes his stuff which only takes up a fourth of the space. "Yeah, I don't need much."

"Clearly," I mutter.

The past six months have been nothing short of wonderful. Devon and I basically jumped headfirst into a full-on relationship. I guess pretending to be dating for a week got a lot of the awkwardness out of the way. We started spending all of our free time together, and although I still had my doubts, he has quieted every one of them.

He's always been patient and understanding. He never pushes me.

I never knew I could love someone as much as him.

I even ran into Alan one day at the mall a couple towns over. We said a pleasant hello, and I went on about my day. There was no bad blood.

I got my closure and a great guy, so I think overall, I ended up with the better part of the deal.

It's funny how things work out in ways that you least expect them too.

Since Devon was basically over here all the time anyway, we decided it would be a good idea for him to move in. He offered to pay half the bills so that I can put more money aside to eventually buy the bar.

Devon offered to just help me pay for it outright, but I'm much too stubborn to go for that, so we worked out this deal instead.

It works well from a financial standpoint; plus, I get to wake up next to him every single morning.

No pillow walls anymore.

At this point, I'm not even sure how I would sleep if I wasn't completely draped across him.

Devon walks over to give me a quick kiss before saying, "I'm going to make us some breakfast."

"I had coffee," I say.

"Coffee isn't breakfast."

I know that, but it's still fun to give him shit.

I continue going through our clothes, trying to get everything in its new spot when suddenly I realize something's missing.

Walking toward the kitchen, I pass Bones and Miss Trixie, Devon's cat, who has become a very *indoor* cat these days. The two have become fast friends and are already snuggled up on the couch together.

So stinking cute.

"Devon," I call. "Did you hide my underwear?"

"I don't know what you're talking about."

"Devon," I groan. "Why do you insist on doing this?"

He's hidden a few pairs before as a joke, but now I can find literally none of them.

I walk over to him, sliding my arms around him from behind.

"If you didn't want me to wear underwear, why didn't you just ask? I would have told you that I'm not wearing any right now."

He quickly turns around and pulls me close. "Really?"

"Really. You don't have to hide them."

"Get in the bedroom," he growls.

"What about breakfast."

"Oh, I'm about to have *my* breakfast. Get on the bed. Now."

I quickly run in there with him hot on my heels.

Ripping off my jeans, he settles between my legs. "How about every time you don't wear panties, I go down on you until you can't take anymore?"

"What if I don't wear them every single day?"

"Then, I do it. Every. Single. Day."

I look down at him smiling.

"Deal."

Also By Stephanie Renee

The Constant Series

A Constant Surprise

A Constant Reminder

A Constant Love

A Constant Christmas

Spin-offs

Seeing Red

Aces Wild

The Grady Series

All the Right Things

All the Right Reasons

All the Right Choices

All the Right Moves

All the Right Moments

All the Right Ideas

All the Right Memories

The Samson Boys

Duke's Redemption
Tanner's Forever
Devon's Deal

Standalone Books

Beauty and the Boss Man

The House Always Wins
Have a Little Faith (Part of the Cinnamon Roll Saviors Collab)

Made in the USA
Middletown, DE
24 October 2023

41347451R00154